Baked and Burned

TORI ROSS

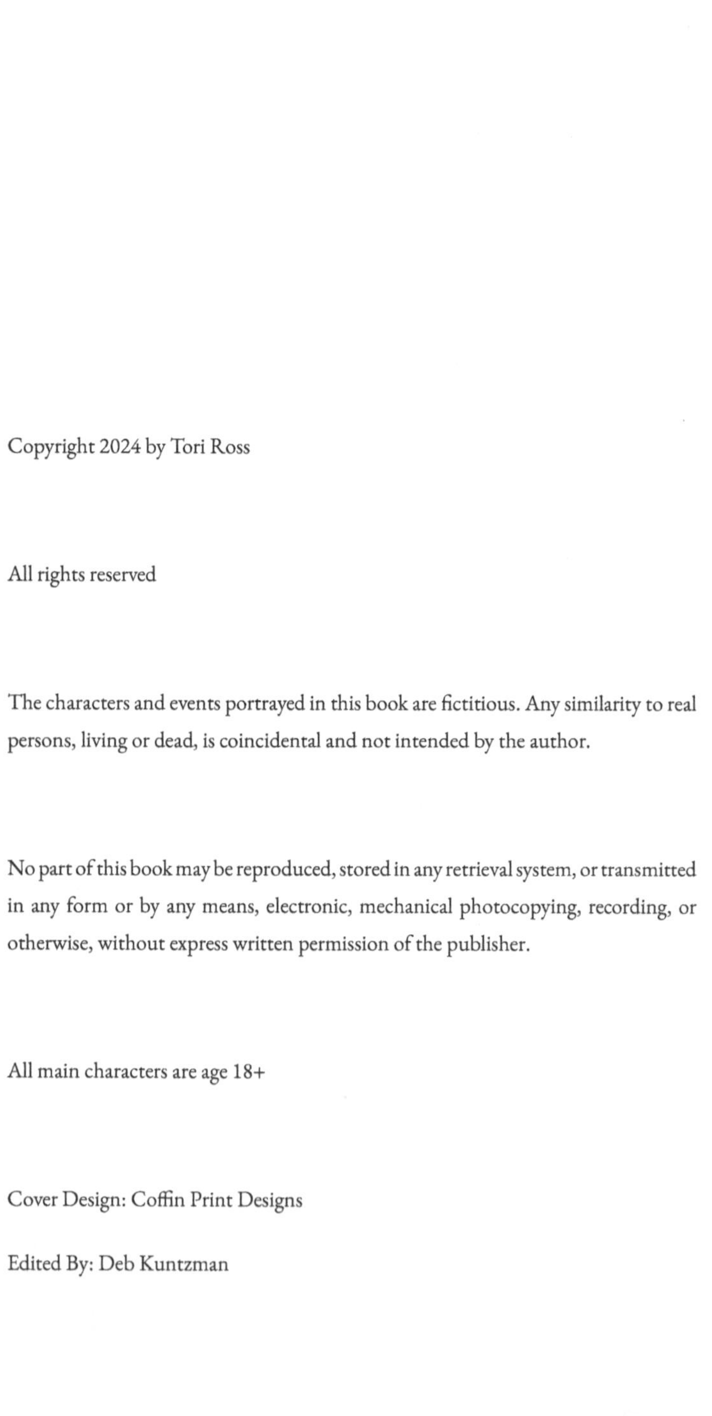

Contents

Author's Note

This book is not for everyone. Hell, *Contact High* wasn't for everyone, but if you loved *Contact High*, you may not like this book. *Contact High* was a rom com about marijuana legalization and the differing opinions on it as a couple fell in love. This is a book about a couple that has a one-night stand, only to find out that a pregnancy has resulted.

Would they fall in love otherwise? I like to think I set that up nicely before they even find out Kailee's pregnant, but I'll let you be the judge.

But...

Be forewarned that this book is raw, real, and shows real choices and feelings in our world.

I didn't write this book like other romance books with babies in them. You have enough of those to choose from where the woman immediately falls in love with her child or immediately loves the idea of being pregnant with one. You have enough to read of a man being happy to be a father as soon as he's told. But in *Baked and Burned* world, a surprise pregnancy doesn't always result in everyone skipping through a meadow and holding hands. I wrote a book about doubt, fear, and navigating a new relationship when something unexpected happens. I wrote a book about love happening in spite of that.

This book may be seen as political in certain places as Kailee rants about her options, but it's not really intended to be. Even so, I live in the real world and know that there will be people mad about things she brings up. My hope is if something (on either side of the coin) strikes home, you sit with it a few minutes and think about why. But one thing about me is that I have big shoulders and even bigger balls, so I decided to give you the story as it came to me. This is the story as it unfolded, and it went completely off outline after about chapter five. Once I got going during the writing process, Kailee told me how she felt. Turns out, she's scared, ill-prepared, and has legitimate medical concerns women face every single day.

Content Warnings: Abortion is discussed as a realistic option in this book, even though Kailee and Chase ultimately decide to go through with the pregnancy. Other content warnings include pregnancy issues like spotting, discussion of high-risk pregnancies, morning sickness, low blood pressure, endometriosis, and post-partum care. You do get a birth scene at the end, but it's not gory. There's a police tasing, and Chase also has bad dreams about something that happened in *Contact High*.

As long as you know this going in, I hope you enjoy the book. It is funny in many places, and I laughed writing it, especially at Liam and Chase, the cake fight, and you'll never look at peanut butter quite the same. It's steamy since I only write books with steam in them. I hope you giggle. I hope you cheer for Kailee and Chase.

If it's not your jam, stop reading right now.

If it's something you're willing to wade into, let's get started.

For the reader at Flirty in Kansas City who said *Contact High* was too spicy, but you'd read the sequel because it was a good story.

Skip the peanut butter scene.

A Few Weeks Ago

KAILEE

"I think we were ditched," the hot guy says, sidling up to me at the bar. He holds out his hand and licks a drop of beer off his bottom lip before looking me up and down. "Chase Barnett. Officer Half Inch's partner. Are you friends with Lorelei?"

I take the outstretched hand and blink twice as I shake it. Is he real? Nobody can be this hot without airbrushing, a personal chef, and a personal trainer. "Kailee," I say. At least, I try to say it. My mouth is still slightly open, and it's hard to talk when my lips won't move properly.

This is Liam's partner?

Liam's a drug task force agent who's been giving my boss and best friend, Lorelei, shit for running a food truck that specializes in marijuana edibles. Even though he's been a prat, they've been eye fucking since they met. Conveniently, I came here tonight with Lorelei, and she ditched me for Liam to drive her home as soon as Liam and Chase walked into the bar.

I hope Lorelei rides Liam like she's Zorro. We could both use a good lay. I could certainly use a good ride on Officer Viking next to me.

He's tall. Not as tall as Liam, but Chase must be a little over six feet. Wide shoulders. Perfectly straight, white teeth with blond curls that stop just past his ears. His ice-blue eyes are staring at me like he's a hungry wolf and my body is a lamb shank.

Fuck. I should have worn something nicer than a simple pair of jeans and a pink, long-sleeved shirt. At least it's a V-neck, and I squeeze my arms at my sides, hoping it pushes my breasts up a little. It works, and Chase flicks his eyes to my breasts, opens his mouth like he wants to talk, and looks away.

Say something, moron. Keep the hot guy talking to you. "I see you picked up on the nickname for your buddy. Is there any way you can get him off Lorelei's ass?"

He smiles and clears his throat. "Well, I'd like to say I could get him off her ass, but I don't think there's any way to keep him away from her ass." He scoots closer to me and tilts his head, studying me for a sign that I'm interested. I know this game. "If you know what I mean."

"You've noticed the constant eye fucking between them?"

"This is the first time I've met her, but in the thirty seconds I was around them both, there was definite eye fucking. He also can't keep his trap shut about her." He takes a sip of his beer and nods at me. "What's your story?"

"I work for Lorelei. I'm in the back of the edibles truck, taking stuff out of the oven and mixing second batches. Thankfully, I haven't been arrested for it by your dick partner yet, unlike Lorelei. Then again, I think he only cuffed her to get her into cuffs at least once."

Chase raises his beer in a salute. "True that. For what it's worth, I think he's being childish. I have no problem with weed since the state legalized it. It's the same legality as beer, for the most part. Maybe a bit stricter."

"I got the frisking he gave her on video. Dare me to put it on YouTube?"

"Maybe not yet since he's my partner. I'd probably get in deep shit with him if he did something wrong, but I like how you think. Points for vindictiveness." He moves closer to me on the stool, and the air practically crackles with sex. My fingers flex around my margarita glass, itching to run my hands up his bicep. "But I wanted to know about you personally. No Liam or Lorelei around. You're beautiful."

Oh. My. Fucking. God. The Viking cop thinks I'm pretty. I'm medium height and a bit curvy except for my lack of butt. We can't all be perfect like the specimen in front of me. Still, I wish I had washed my hair and done something with it besides a ponytail. I don't wear much makeup, and I suddenly long for more than just a hit of mascara and lip gloss on my face.

Is it just my imagination or are his pupils dark? His chest heaves under his shirt. It's blue, like his eyes. Maybe my ponytail and lack of makeup don't matter as much as the cosmetics industry would have us think.

And why does he keep biting his lip? It's all I can do to not clear the bar in one swipe of my arm, pull him to the scratched wood, and pull his dick out of those jeans he's wearing. I could really use some physical affection, and this guy may be just the ticket.

I take a deep breath, grounding myself and readying myself at the same time. He leans closer and touches a small wisp of dark hair that's escaped my ponytail. He doesn't even touch my skin, but I shiver, goosebumps moving up my arms. His eyes study my face, and he smiles when his eyes lock on a small beauty mark mole at the bottom of my cheek. I've always liked it and most people don't even notice it, but I touch the spot, suddenly self-conscious.

Pushing the thought aside, I force my mouth to open so he doesn't think I'm an idiot. Act cool, Kailee. Keep it together.

"My name is Kailee Lipshitz, and yes, my nickname in high school was Shits. I just like to put that out there first thing so everyone can laugh and move past it. I work at a weed truck on the side but mostly pay the bills by substitute teaching. My favorite food is corndogs. I like punk rock from fifteen years before I was born, and my pet peeves include reality TV and the word *moist*."

He stares directly into my eyes. "I'm Chase Barnett. I hunt drug dealers for a living and have a douche partner with an overactive tape measure." He points to his shirt. "My favorite color is blue, and I promise never to say the word moist around you unless I'm describing cake. I also have a dragon tattoo up my right thigh that curls toward my dick, and I very much want to show it to you."

"You want to show me your dragon tattoo or your dick?"

He growls, his lip curling a little. He actually fucking growls as he leans even closer to me. "Both."

I put my finger in the air to get the bartender's attention. "Check please!"

***

I can't get a great glimpse of that dick he wanted to show me with my hands splayed against his beige kitchen wall as he takes me from behind. His dick is huge, though. I feel that all on my own without having to see it.

He drove us to his apartment, and I didn't even get to look at anything past his entryway and a small desk off to the side. I did a quick, cursory search for pictures of girlfriends before he had me up against the wall, kissing me with hunger. There are no signs of a lady in the apartment, and he tastes like beer and man – a deadly combination.

It was all a blur how we got this far. His hands roamed every part of my body before flicking my shirt somewhere near the front door and unhooking my bra in one experienced flick of his fingers. As he backed me into the kitchen, we both gave up aiming for his bedroom, and he spun me around, pulled my jeans down my body, nudged my legs apart, and took me right up against his wall, pushing himself into me with one urgent thrust.

Now, my cheek sticks to the cool wall, and it's a nice contrast to the heat of him at my back. He grips my hips hard, so hard there will be fingerprints tomorrow. I also know I'll trace the marks with my own finger pads for days, trying to remember every single moment of him. Reaching down, I rub my clit like a frantic madwoman, pushing myself to a much-needed orgasm.

He pulls my hair and jerks my head back so hard my neck muscles scream. "That's it, sweetheart. Make yourself come on my dick." He nuzzles my neck, and I swear my pussy gets wetter at his breath on my jaw. "I'm going to make you come all night."

I don't doubt his words. He's using and abusing my pussy so much that I can't catch my breath. My forehead bangs into his wall so hard that a nearby kitschy picture of a rooster in a chef's hat falls to the floor. We don't comment on it or move to pick it up. Chase kicks it aside as he widens his stance even more, notices I may be uncomfortable against the wall, and shifts me to the nearby kitchen counter.

I'm bent at the waist, and he purrs at my bent-over form. Reaching around, he palms my breasts as I continue flicking my clit just the way I like it. "God, these fucking tits are gorgeous. Mind if I fuck them later?" he asks breathlessly.

"Knock yourself out," I grunt as his cock hits all the way home again, pushing me into the granite. "Sounds like a great way to see that tattoo you talked up."

He chuckles and smacks my ass with one hand while still holding onto a breast. "Baby girl, you're going to be so familiar with my tattoo and dick before I'm done with you tonight that you'll be able to describe it to a sketch artist. I hope you have bags of frozen peas to take good care of this tight, little box tomorrow."

Electric pleasure moves up my spine, and I squirm against him as he laughs. "I love making gorgeous women squirm on my dick."

The nasty words from his mouth pushes me over the edge, and my orgasm hits so hard it's like slamming into a fun wall. This is no wave-like orgasm you can surf and catch your breath between crests. This is an eye-rolling, mind-losing release I'll remember for the rest of my life.

My pussy tenses around him, milking his cock and enticing him to buck harder into me. Someone in the room is moaning a million cuss words. I think that person's me, but he's also cussing, and our words blend together. Whoever's moaning so loud knows a lot of dirty words, though, and they sound sexy as fuck when they grunt them.

Sweat drips from somewhere on his body and lands on my back before dribbling straight down my butt crack. Chase, the sick bastard, sees it, swipes a finger through the sweat to wipe it away, and then makes a sucking noise. Did he just suck the sweat that was in my butt crack off his finger?

The sheer filth of it makes me come again. I haven't come back-to-back in five years without a vibrator. It's my own finger doing the clitoral stimulation, but damn if having a gorgeous man fucking me just right doesn't heighten every sense I have.

My second orgasm does it for Chase, and he grips my waist, pulling me against him in long, quick thrusts. I can't catch my breath, and I push my forehead to his counter, thinking about how full of him I am.

He releases deep inside of me with a long groan. As soon as his cock stops twitching, he pulls out and massages my ass as he bends down to kiss my hip. He drops more kisses on my lower back and works his way up my body, subtly telling me he's not yet done with me for the night.

"Are you staying in my bed so I can watch my cum run out of you all night?" he asks. He drops a kiss on the nape of my neck and then moves so his jaw is next to my ear. "You can wear my Nickelback t-shirt."

How can a girl say no to that?

Present Day

CHASE

The nightmare is always the same. In the dream, Liam's being strangled by Jacob Lambert, the drug dealer we're busting, and there's blood everywhere. So much fucking blood. Why was there so much blood? I don't know if it's my partner's blood or Jacob's, but I don't think about it too long. I was taught to react to a situation in the moment, and I can only think about my own reaction.

Like it's slow motion, I raise my weapon, yell something at Lambert to get the fuck off Liam, and move into the room. Jacob doesn't listen and keeps strangling Liam.

I fire my weapon. The shot lands where I placed it in Lambert's shoulder blade to get him to let go. Unfortunately, Lambert's hyped on his own product, so the bullet doesn't faze him. Liam goes still under him, and I panic, even as Lambert doesn't let go of Liam. Seeing my best friend stop fighting for his life and go still does things to me.

I fire a second shot into the back of Lambert's head. Blood sprays everywhere against the wall Lambert was facing and all over Liam.

As Lambert soundlessly slumps forward on top of my friend, I force my feet to move and check on Liam. Rolling Lambert's body to the side, Liam doesn't make a sound. There's no breath. Nothing. The silence in the room is deafening, the only sound in my ears is the ringing from the shots fired in a contained room.

It all happened exactly like that, except Liam doesn't survive in my dream. I did CPR and got him breathing again in real life, even if I'll never tell him I did it. He'll never get over knowing I did mouth-to-mouth resuscitation. He would probably give me shit about me finally getting to tongue him and having to wait to do it until he was half dead, and I don't want to listen to the bullshit.

It all worked out for him in reality, but the dream stays with me.

What would I have done if I had lost him that night?

Morning light seeps through my curtains, and I swing my legs off the bed, already pumped full of adrenaline the way I feel every time I have the nightmare. I look over on the other side of the bed and wonder if I was drunk enough last night to pick up a woman for some fun. If I picked up a good time, she's gone.

There's no one in my bed and no rustling sound of a woman going through my kitchen cabinets in search of cereal or granola bars.

She wouldn't be the first that didn't stay for breakfast if she existed at all. I probably slept alone last night.

I get out of bed and pad to the bathroom. After taking a piss, brushing my teeth, and rolling deodorant on the important parts, I slip into my standard-issue work clothes and place the police badge on my belt. I comb my unruly hair into something presentable and flick the bathroom light off to search for coffee.

Today's an office day, which means mandatory counseling and meetings about firing my weapon and killing a suspect. I'd rather eat glass than go through any of it, but it's necessary. Liam also has to go through it when he gets back from medical leave. He's still healing from a few wounds and in physical therapy for a shoulder injury. Technically, we're cleared to work once his physical issue is fixed as long as we agree to attend counseling for a few months, but I don't want to take any new cases without him. It's been a rough few weeks with me being evaluated both physically and mentally to even make sure I'm ready to ride a desk or fill in where needed.

Thankfully, there's a temporary opening for a school resource officer that will keep me busy until Liam gets back, and I'm being briefed on it this afternoon, complete with a tour of the high school.

This will be great. Fine. Fantastic. I can simply show up to the school, talk to the kids and teachers, and make sure they're safe simply by being present in the building. It'll be a relaxing change of pace. I won't have to do stakeouts in the middle of the night or chart drug buys and do tons of paperwork.

Most people don't know that police work is mostly paperwork or simply watching cases build.

I'll go to work, come home, and maybe pop over to Liam's for a beer if he's not with Lorelei.

OK, I'll be drinking beer by myself. I couldn't pry him away from Lorelei now if I tried. They're glued to the hip, especially since Liam finally got his head out of his ass and told Lorelei he loves her.

I'm actually surprised they're not married yet.

I should go out, pick up a woman, and bring her home for a quick fuck. A one-night stand is exactly what I need.

Too bad I can't enjoy one-night stands anymore, and it has nothing to do with work.

I haven't enjoyed one since *her*.

Her name swims in my foggy pre-coffee brain. Kailee. Kailee Lipshitz. Lorelei's best friend. The one-night stand I wanted more time with. I wanted a two-night stand. Something about her makes me want a forever stand. She's the type of girl I've always wanted. She's beautiful, kept up with my stupid banter, and practically melted into me the night we were together. She obviously has a good friend in Lorelei, and if Lorelei vouches for her, I know she's a good person.

It's not just her name and face that swim in my mind. It's everything. I haven't been able to get the taste of her salty skin off my tongue since we fucked like rabbits in my kitchen weeks ago. Her touch. Her mouth on my cock in the middle of the night as she licked and cooed over my tattoo and swallowed every drop I gave her. The way her clit tasted like waffles when I lapped it like a maniac after she was done with me. The way she fucked me again in my bed in the wee hours of the morning.

I also can't stop thinking about the way she slipped out and must have taken an Uber home before I woke. That burns most of all.

***

"Here's the gym," the principal says, waving his hand at the polished wood floor and basketball hoops like they're prizes on *The Price is Right*. "You'll need to walk through every now and then during physical education classes just to be seen. It's a good time for the kids to come up and talk since they're just doing exercises or playing sports. The cafeteria is also a great place to wander during lunches. We want you to be seen and interact with the students."

I nod and smile. I'm already looking forward to that aspect of the job. It'll be a welcome change to talk to students and teachers who aren't drug dealers. That's the only interaction I get at my normal job – drug dealers, the dealers' girlfriends, or other cops. Other cops are fine to talk about work, but they aren't always the best friend choices. Liam's a safe choice as a buddy, but cops have statistically higher rates of depression, alcoholism, and anxiety. The guys in my department aren't exactly golf buddies. We can be drinking buddies on a random Thursday, but it doesn't go deeper.

It even smells nicer in this building. Cleaner. The taxpayers fund a nice HVAC system, and everything is well-maintained by the janitorial staff. It certainly doesn't smell like suspect body odor or ceiling mildew. I won't be in a stuffy bullpen with other sweaty officers as they hide their pit stains seeping through their dress shirts while investigating criminals and drinking bad coffee.

There's even a nice self-serve coffee machine in the teacher's lounge I can use. No more vending coffee out of paper cups. They have a swivel carousel of coffee pods, and I spent ten minutes this morning debating between flavors like buttered rum and mocha marshmallow.

"Follow me, and I'll take you down to our electives section of the building," Principal Richter says, waving at me to follow him.

As he walks and prattles on about the staff bathroom and janitor closet, I take in the surroundings.

It's a modern school, just built in the last ten years. It's led by a younger principal who's more into aesthetics and maintaining a good appearance to make the students want to come to school. He probably got the job because of his doctorate in education and the ability to relate with younger students, not because he was the most tenured.

I'm a straight man, but I'd say Jeff Richter is a handsome guy. His hair is like mine – not brown, but not all the way blond either. His skin is tan like he just got back from a cruise, and he's runner lean. Although he's a couple inches shorter, his shoulders are as wide as mine. I should invite him out for drinks sometime. He may be a good wingman for pussy pickup now that Liam's taken. He can't be older than thirty-five, and it's weird to see a principal around my age. When I was a kid, they always seemed so old.

Then again, I was in the principal's office a lot. I'm sure my high school principal looked haggard because he was tired as fuck of seeing me in his office for doing stupid shit like getting blown in the janitor's closet.

"You have the electives separate from the main classes?" I ask, curious.

"Yeah, it's the classes that aren't standard. You know, math and science have their own department areas. This hallway contains classes like band, choir, and industrial tech."

"Industrial tech?"

He waves his hand like he's annoyed. "It's shop. I don't know why they make it sound so fancy now."

He points further down the hall, mumbling something about child development classes where the students take home a mechanical baby with a chip in it that registers if the baby gets shaken to keep it from crying. I'm not listening, though. I'm too busy staring through a classroom window and watching a goddess stir something with a hand mixer.

The goddess's hair is up in a smooth ponytail with a curly swish at the end. She speaks to the student she's helping and smiles easily at them like she was born to teach. She's in black, fitted dress pants and a button-down shirt with a Peter Pan collar. She's not wearing much makeup since she's working with students, but her natural beauty and long lashes are stunning.

I step to the door and press my face to the glass so hard that if she looked over, she'd probably see my nose scrunched up like a pig's nose as I fog up the glass. My eyes are so wide I momentarily wonder if they'll pop out of my skull.

Jeff comes up behind me and stands on his tiptoes, looking over my shoulder. "Oh, yeah. The sub."

"Sub?" I ask, my heart pounding. My mouth is dry, and I squeak the word.

"She's filling in for our pastry and baking teacher who's out for knee surgery. Just started Monday. Personally, I don't think she knows shit, but well, subs are in short supply."

"She knows the basics," I say, flexing my hands that the first thing the principal mentioned was something negative.

"How do you know?"

"She helps run a baking food truck."

"Do you know her?" he asks, and I turn to look at him, finally tearing my eyes away from Kailee. Something about his voice irritates me, and I know then that this guy is not my new wing-man. "Because if you know her, I'd love a friendly, non-working introduction. We've only talked professional stuff."

I clear my throat, flexing my hands and shoving them in my pockets so I don't knock this dick into the wall. "Not that well," I say. Think, dumb ass. "Well, I know her well enough to know what she does for a living. My friend dates her boss."

Jeff smiles a leering smile toward the classroom window. What a fucking douche.

"I think she's a lesbian," I say a little louder than I should. A passing student on the way back from the bathroom stops and glances at us before widening their eyes, shaking their head, and moving on.

"Oh, that sucks," Jeff says.

I can't believe he's talking so unprofessionally about her. Sure, I want to go in there and push her over the counter like I did a few weeks ago and unbutton her professional, button-down shirt with my teeth, but I'm not going to act on it here.

"It sucks because I need to tell Leo," Richter whispers behind me.

"Leo?"

"The industrial tech teacher. We have a bet going on who can get her panties off first," he says, looking back through the window. Part of me wants to push his face through the glass.

I grit my teeth in anger and jealousy even as my heart pounds out of my chest with excitement to see her. I look back through the window, not really caring if she sees me. If that happens, I'll run to her like I'm running in slow-motion, my arms out. My dick practically knocks at my zipper. It's such a Pavlovian response. It's like my cock knows exactly what this woman is capable of.

Great. I just told her boss, albeit a temporary one, that she's a lesbian. There's nothing wrong with being a lesbian, but she's definitely into guys in some way if the way she rode my dick was any indication. I panicked.

"Hey, we could let you into the bet," Principal Dick Weasel mutters behind me.

I turn again and force a smile. The asshole practically pants with male bonding and the promise of a challenge. I'm stuck here for a few weeks, and I shouldn't piss off the guy who let me work here. I also don't need it getting back to my chief that I wasn't exactly a team player.

"Not my thing, but good luck," I say, hating myself as soon as the words leave my mouth. I shouldn't even wish these dick-bags luck. I should say something – stick up for all women everywhere. I just stuff my hands in my pockets and stare at him. It's a police tactic to get people talking while I make them uncomfortable with silence.

"That's OK. I'll duke it out with Leo," he says with a chuckle. He slaps me on the back, and I turn back to stare at her again.

Too bad for these assholes I already won their stupid bet weeks ago when Kailee Lipshitz's panties were on my kitchen floor, and I'm not about to enter into something so juvenile with a guy wearing pleated pants. It wouldn't be fair to anyone.

Chapter 3

KAILEE

"Who can tell me what this is?" I ask, holding up a red instrument that, truth be told, looks like a butt plug.

I legit don't have a clue what this instrument is. I thought it would be best to ask the students in a voice that sounds like I'm quizzing them. One hand is in my pocket with my fingers crossed, desperately hoping a student knows what it is so I don't look like an ass when it comes time to explain it.

Thankfully, one mousy young lady at the second prep table raises her hand. I point at her, and she adjusts her tortoise-shell glasses before she answers. "It's a strawberry huller. My mom uses them for chocolate-filled strawberries."

I look closer at the object and squint. There's a pointed tip and a round button at the base. When I click it, the pointed tip retracts.

Huh. Interesting.

"Wonderful. What else could we make with hulled strawberries?"

A few hands go up, and I call on them, mentally heaving a sigh of relief.

I am way over my head here. I work in a baking food truck, but I'm learning that I have no idea about the correct way to do things in baking. I put ingredients in a mixer, pop stuff in the oven, and take it out when I work with Lorelei on the truck. I wash my hands before I touch anything. I keep my hair out of the food. Simple.

Apparently, making pretty pastry requires knowing a bunch of methods I've never heard of. I had to Google what it meant to fold an ingredient into dough. Don't get me started on finding the best method to separate egg whites. We don't work with many egg whites on the truck because cannabutter has a greenish tint that makes white batter appear green. Most of our food requires the entire egg and is chocolate or in bread form.

This gig is only for a few months until Janice Corbitt, baking teacher extraordinaire, can recover from a knee replacement. The high school needed a sub, and they couldn't find a single person with a Family and Consumer Science certification to take the gig. Technically, it's subbing and only temporary. It's also education. There's not a line out the door for taking this job.

The district requires that a long-term substitute be a certified teacher with any type of certificate. I have an early childhood certificate I don't use. It's not exactly a great fit here, and I'm still intimidated by students who are the size of professional athletes. I've also never dealt with students who have the facial hair of a middle-aged man.

At least the kids are potty-trained at this level.

Mostly.

I have seniors that couldn't give a shit about anything. Most of them have their graduation requirements and their college acceptance letters in hand. Any senior in this class, except for the one student who mentioned he's going to culinary school when he graduates, is simply biding their time. I should let him teach on days I don't feel like it.

I divide the group into cooking teams of four and go through the ingredients necessary to make strawberry shortcake from scratch, including whipped cream, and then have the mousy student demonstrate the strawberry huller for decorative straw-berries on the top. They go to work without much direction other than the recipe card at each table that one person on each team reads aloud to their group members. That's another perk of seniors. They're mostly self-sufficient.

Ms. Corbitt had lesson plans already in place because she's taught this class for almost thirty years. It's a dream gig to come in every day, set out ingredients and recipe cards, remind the students of cooking safety, take attendance, and make sure no students get hurt and no furniture gets broken. She also teaches sewing, but it's not on my schedule this quarter. That's a relief since I can't even sew a button.

I do a cursory walk around the room, oohing and ahhing over the students' hard work. Then, I walk to the teacher's desk and sit, resisting the urge to put my head on the desk and take a nap. I'm used to being on my feet and circling the room as a sub, but I can't work up the energy with this gig.

I chalk up my lack of energy to the window situation in the room. Windows are required for ventilation in any class that uses stoves, but they don't get sun at any point. I'm used to taking elementary kids out for recess or stepping out of Lorelei's truck for some sun and fresh air when I'm at work. Even when I can't step out, the back door of the truck can be opened. This place is a dungeon with a nice hint of vanilla.

My eyes almost droop closed until a knock at the classroom door startles me, forcing my eyes open. The students turn to the person in the window, always curious, and I get up to unlock the door I always keep locked for safety.

I know it's a man, but I can't see his face because of the small window. Hopefully, it's not Principal Richter. I was almost asleep on the desk and don't want to get in trouble.

I swing the door open and find Leo Paulson in front of me with a smile on his face. "Hi, Kailee." He clears his throat and looks at the students behind me. "Um, Ms. Lipshitz."

A student behind me laughs like at least one of them does every time someone says my last name. I tell them to use Ms. L. when they need me. I did that on my second day here since I was already tired of them calling me Ms. Shits.

"Hi, Leo. What's up?" I ask, darting my eyes left and right. Why's he over here?

I look across the hall to his classroom and don't see any students, but I hear them. I'm fairly certain he has freshmen this hour. Someone works a saw or another power tool. A drill? "Shouldn't you be in the classroom if a student is using a power tool?"

"Probably," he says. He waves his hands like he can't be fucked with students and power tools. "I just wanted to say hi."

Well, this is awkward. I look back at my own students, who all look down at their shortcake mixture at the same time. Subtle.

"Uh...hi," I say.

He leans closer to me and drops his voice. "I also wanted to ask you to dinner tonight." He nods for a moment. "With me."

I move an inch or two back from him. "Are you asking me on a date?"

"Yes," he says, biting his lip and wringing his hands.

Lord, have mercy on my soul. I give Leo a cursory glance. He's not bad looking. He has a job, a pension, and all of his hair. It's prematurely graying because he's salt and pepper, but he can't be older than thirty-eight or so. He's fit with a wide chest, and I swear he flexes his pecs under his golf shirt while I study him.

He's a great guy on paper.

He's also awkward as fuck, and I'm not quite sure I've ever seen him blink.

Somewhere in the back of my mind, I hear Lorelei's voice. "Kailee, you can't judge a man by one weird quirk. If he's nice and isn't a troll living in a box under a bridge, he's worth a conversation. Sometimes, the nice guys are worth getting to know."

I inhale through my nose and immediately gag on the smell of the dairy product for whipped topping. It's so thick it practically chokes me. I cover my nose with my forearm and act like I'm simply wiping my nose, trying not to retch. I should open a window.

Leo doesn't notice. He stands in front of me, his left foot tapping against the linoleum. This isn't Tinder. This is an opportunity to go out with a man that I don't have to use technology to find. Not that there's anything wrong with Tinder, but sometimes I wish I could meet men in person before deciding if I want to go out with them.

He's not ugly. He has a good job, tenure, and doesn't live at home with his mother. He talked about recently buying a house when I first met him. He's a little awkward, and I'm not sure I have a lot of chemistry with him, but that can grow, right? It's not like I even have to sleep with him. He's a date. I don't have to shave my legs or wax my lady bits. He's not even a one-night stand.

One-night stand…

I sigh and slump against the door frame, and it has nothing to do with Leo Paulson. The idea of a one-night stand isn't appealing anymore.

Not since Chase.

I can't stop thinking about him. Part of me itches to ask Lorelei to get his number from Liam. The other part of me tells me I don't have the strength of heart to play with his kind of horsepower. Keeping up with him in bed that night was exhausting. I've never been laid like that, and the fact that he's a friend of Lorelei's boyfriend threw me off. If it didn't work out between us, we'd be damned to a lifetime of Christmas parties, sharing godchildren, and summer cookouts with the two of them. Who needs to share those things with an ex-boyfriend you can never lift out of your life? It's going to be awkward enough to do all of those things knowing how hard I came on his dick.

He's also another man with a great job, albeit dangerous if Liam's injuries are any clue, and he has benefits and owns an entire house.

A whole real house! Not one of those tiny houses. Not a house he rents and shares with four other people. I don't even know what to do with that information in this housing market.

I tossed and turned in bed with him that night, worried I'm not good enough for him. I'm pretty, but he's a Viking god and a hero of the community, for fuck's sake. He literally hunts drug dealers for a living. He could have way more interesting women than a substitute teacher who scrapes to pay the bills with two jobs and has to join the government health care exchange if she wants a pap smear. If I enter into a relationship with him and it goes bad, will I fuck up my friendship with Lorelei?

I panicked and left him before he woke that morning. I slipped out of his warm bed, gathered my clothing, and dressed at the front door before calling an Uber to take me back to the bar so I could get my car.

I must have pissed him off or not impressed him at all. Lorelei hasn't mentioned him except to tell me that Chase saved Liam during a bust. My ovaries nearly exploded when she told me how Chase saved Liam's life in a bad situation, basically bringing Liam back from the dead. But I need to get over Chase Barnett. I may have to see him when I'm with Lorelei and Liam, but I'll deal with that then. I can't piss my whole youth away because of a guy with good dick game.

I startle, remembering Leo in front of me. Standing up straight, I bat my eyes and force a smile on my face. "Give me your number."

Chapter 4

CHASE

I've been avoiding her for two days. Granted, I've been busy as fuck with learning staff and student names as well as routines. I wander around the tables at lunch, talk to the students, and make small talk with the principal who oversees lunch. I've also been avoiding her hallway like the plague. If Principal Dick Bag has noticed I don't go down that hallway and always spend time in the math and science department, he hasn't said anything.

I've only had one close call with running into her. I was walking through the shelves in the library and thinking about picking up a book to read for the weekend. They have a great selection of comic books for some reason. The librarian, an older woman who looks me from top to bottom every time I come in, said I could borrow school library books on my employee ID the school issued me. I was in the comic section when I heard her voice practically singing a hello to the librarian. They made small talk for a couple of minutes about a fellow staff member's birthday party.

I watched her every move as she went to the small cookbook section, thumbed through a few books until she found what she needed, and left as fast as she arrived. At least I didn't have to duck behind a bunch of shelves like I would have if she was looking for a comic book.

Walking into the cafeteria, I stop short, looking around the area and squinting. The place is usually buzzing with student voices and the clatter of trays. Now, only the janitor pushes a broom along the tile floor, cleaning up wrappers and used sandwich bags. I look at my watch and check the time. This is normally lunch. Where is everyone?

A science teacher walks by, and I stop her. "Excuse me. This is lunchtime, right?"

The science teacher, a middle-aged woman who licks her lips whenever I speak to her, wets her lips like usual and looks at her own watch. "It's early release Wednesday, Officer Barnett. We get out an hour early on Wednesdays. It's to give department teachers time to collaborate. The times for lunch change on those days. They didn't tell you that?"

Shit. I was hoping to grab a burger from the lunch ladies, but a peek inside the kitchen doorway shows them putting things inside the industrial fridge and washing dishes. "They didn't, but thank you," I say to the teacher. "I guess it's the teacher's lounge vending machine today."

She smiles as I walk past her, and my neck feels hot the entire way down the hall like it does when I feel eyes on me. I know the teacher watches my ass cheeks as I walk away, but I don't dare turn around and encourage her.

I push the door open to the teacher's lounge and freeze. My eyes widen when I find Kailee sitting at the table with a spoonful of soup frozen halfway to her mouth. She stares at me with eyes the size of quarters. We're mirror images as we study at each other in numbing silence. Her mouth is open because it was already open for her food. Mine is open because I want to say something but can't form words.

Should I back out? Greet her like everything is fine?

She's wearing a Metallica t-shirt today with a black blazer thrown over it and buttoned. Her hair is pulled back in a messy bun, and she looks like she went out last night. She almost looks hungover. Did she go out with another man? Lorelei? Another friend I don't know?

I run my hand down my dress shirt and adjust the badge attached to my belt. Hopefully, I can smooth out any wrinkles. I shaved today, but I didn't spend much time with my hair. Why didn't I spend time on my appearance? Fuck. Of all days.

"Ch-Chase?" she stammers, shaking her head like she's not sure if I'm real. A piece of hair falls in front of her face with the movement, and my fingers itch to push it behind her ear. "What the hell are you doing here?"

I clear my throat and twist my lips into a smile for her. "I work here for a few weeks. I'm sure you know what happened to Liam."

"Yeah," she drawls.

"Well, there are procedures for after we use our service weapon." She stares at me like I have two heads. "I used my piece." I grimace as soon as the words leave my mouth. This is a woman who knows I can use my piece. I cough into my fist. "I mean, I used my service weapon. There's counseling and...shit we have to do. Paperwork. I'm cleared to fill in where needed until Liam and I can resume our cases."

I'm rambling.

"I walk around," I say, putting my hands on my hips and nodding while I look around the room. I can't look at her and speak correctly. My dick throbs in my pants, and I wish she'd shut her mouth because I want to stick my cock right into the wet hole. "I talk to teachers and kids. You know...making sure you're all safe."

That's it! I'll make her believe I'm heroic and here to make sure she doesn't get hurt. Will she like me then?

Crickets.

I clap my hands. "What are you doing here?" I ask, already knowing the answer.

"I'm teaching pastry and baking while the regular teacher has knee surgery." She blinks and shakes her head again like she's still unsure if I'm real and standing in front of her. When she opens her eyes wide again, a blush crawls up her face.

I know what she's going to say, but I beat her to it. "It's no big deal."

She pauses, closes her mouth, and swallows. "What's no big deal?"

I look past her, making sure no other teachers are around. "We fucked. It was fun. You left the next morning without even leaving a lipstick note on the bathroom mirror. I get it. It's cool. We're fine," I say, swiping my hand like I'm flicking away a spiderweb.

It's definitely not fine. She grips the round table with both hands, her soup forgotten. "I'm sorry about that, Chase. I guess I woke up and panicked about what to say the next day. I'm sure you understand it's awkward."

"Yeah, but we work together now. We also have mutual friends, so I'm sure we can't avoid each other forever. I mean, if Lorelei and Liam ever get married, we'll have to deal with each other at the wedding and during the process before the wedding – bachelor and bachelorette parties, showers, and rehearsals."

I'm rambling, but it's true. We'll be around each other constantly if shit gets serious with Liam and Lorelei. Not just for weddings, either. Brunches, Christmas, promotion parties if Liam ever ranks up, and ski vacations come to mind. I'll see her at every event, and I'll have to deal with my balls throbbing for her warm mouth at every turn.

She chews on the inside of her cheek and nods. "You're right. If you need this table, I can leave."

I look at the open seats around the table. "Um, there's plenty of room."

She blows out a sigh. "I don't want you to feel awkward."

"I'm not awkward." I've seen this woman's bare pussy and sucked on her tits while she rode my dick. I've moaned this woman's name – loudly – and will now attempt to eat a bag of chips and a candy bar next to her while trying not to do anything stupid. Nothing awkward about that. "I can be an adult if you can."

She shrugs and looks down at her soup. Cream of potato, from the looks of it. There's also a tuna salad sandwich on white with lettuce and a sliced tomato next to the soup. An oatmeal cookie is partially wrapped in a napkin, and an apple core sits on the edge of her plate. I walk to the vending machine, suddenly aware of every move my body makes.

She jolts a little when I sit down across from her in the furthest seat I can get, and I busy myself with opening the Snickers bar from the machine. After chewing and swallowing, I look at her. "What have you been up to?"

"Stuff."

I take another bite. "What kind of stuff?" I ask.

"Stuff kind of stuff."

I finish my candy bar in a few more bites and start on my Doritos. "Did I do something wrong?"

She finally looks up. "I beg your pardon?"

"That night. Did I do something to make you leave so fast, not say goodbye, and now we can't have a civil conversation? Like...was it bad? You can tell me if it was. I'm open to improvement. I've never thought to send out a survey afterward, but now that I think about it, that may be a good thing for men to do. Was I such a bad fuck that you'll never speak to me again and I should hold my head in shame?"

She reddens and looks back down before picking up her sandwich and biting into it. Once she's done chewing, she furrows her brow and looks at me with a wounded look. Fuck. I missed the clit that night. She faked it. I'm about to hear how I'm the worst lay she's ever had. I make an effort to not squeeze the bag of chips until every chip in the bag is mush.

She sniffs. "It was good. That's why I panicked. It was...too good, Chase."

I tilt my head. "You ran away because I fucked you right? Jesus Christ, I've never heard of that. You usually hear of the opposite problem."

"Look, I'm not used to guys knowing what to do and actually being...." She trails off and waves her hand at me. "I'm not used to guys being all hot and having jobs that have benefits with 401ks and being able to find the G spot. You know...stuff?"

"I didn't realize that my taxpayer-funded dental plan was that big of a turnoff. What kind of douche canoes do you date?"

"I don't date guys like you!" she yells. My eyes flick to the side entrance of the lounge, hoping the office secretaries can't hear us.

"Guys like me? You mean guys that can show a girl what she's missing and not even get a kiss goodbye?" I have no idea why I'm so grouchy. Those words came out harsher than I wanted. What is it with her? Why does she get me riled up more than other women? I've had numerous one-night stands, and I couldn't care less what they thought of me. With her, it's like I'm playing in the sex Olympics, and I'm desperately trying to impress the Russian judge on the dismount.

"I date punk band drummers and guys that have hot air balloon businesses that last a month. There was one graphic designer, which is a respectable gig, but he was freelance and still lived with his mother. You have a house, a car that doesn't smell like vomit, and you're...well, you're you."

"I didn't ask you to marry me. I just thought we could make toast together the next morning. Maybe some herbal tea or some flavored coffee. You didn't even let me wow you with my creamer collection."

Kailee stands and wads up her half-eaten sandwich. "I can see that we just need to remain professional while we're here. And don't worry about Lorelei and Liam. If we're at their house or at dinner, I'll be nothing but sweet to you. I'm just not comfortable with doing more than that."

"Because I'm too good of a catch?" I let out a low whistle. "Wow. Someone has a self-esteem problem, and it's not me."

She ignores my comment, tosses her lunch trash in the bin, and walks out of the teacher's lounge, shutting the door a little harder than necessary.

Chapter 5

KAILEE

"You have a self-esteem problem," Lorelei says, putting banana bread ingredients into the stand mixer and turning it on.

We're working an adult birthday party on someone's private farmland. A food truck that sells pub food and beer is parked across from us, and partygoers come and go, grabbing samples and food between the two trucks, some of them stopping and remarking they've never tried a marijuana edible. Lorelei hands out some business cards that advertise private parties and events like festivals and concerts, but our focus is getting food out to the ravenous partygoers. The party planner pre-paid us for all food and ingredients, so we're both working the baking aspect and not having to fuck with a cash register. The only thing we have to do by law is scan the ID of anyone wanting something from the truck and make sure we only serve them a full-sized dessert once or a couple of minuscule samples. It's against the law to give them more than a certain amount.

If we run afoul of the rules, Liam comes to spank Lorelei.

"That seems to be the consensus," I say. I don't look at her as I pull brownies out of the oven. Wiping my face on my apron, I set the brownies on the cooling rack and grab a bottle of water, downing it in one go. "Is it hotter than usual in here?"

Lorelei shrugs. "It's unseasonably warm out. I'll open the back door. Don't think you're going to change the subject on me, though. Spill. Did you go out with the shop teacher?"

I sigh and lean against the counter as I open another bottle of water. "Not yet. I was supposed to go out the night he asked me, but I got home and just wanted to curl up in pajamas and never leave again. I texted him and rescheduled. We go out next weekend."

"So, you just didn't feel like it? Isn't that a bad sign?"

"What do you mean?" I ask.

"If you like a guy, you should be chomping at the bit to see him. I know I can't wait to see Liam every night now. It's almost painful to go to work."

I make a gagging gesture and roll my eyes. "Yes. I forgot. Liam, who you hated with the fire of a thousand nuclear reactors two months ago, is now a mythological savior. He's everything you wanted in a man, and his dick tastes like powdered sugar."

Lorelei throws a dish towel at me, and I catch it with one hand. "I'm just saying that I'd like you to find a guy you couldn't wait to be in the same room with."

"What is it with people who are newly in love? They want everyone coupled up."

"It wouldn't hurt you to get out and mingle."

"I am. I'm going out with Leo next weekend." I give her a side-eyed look. "Unless you need me to work the metal concert with you. I mean, you'll be busy. You'll need an extra set of hands."

"Nope. Not going to weasel out of a date with a nice guy. Liam can help me. Nola's offered to help now that she's feeling better and on her feet.

Nola is Liam's mother and fighting cancer. Her chemo just ended, and the doctors say she's on the upswing. She's going to make it. Nola and Lorelei were fast friends and adore each other. Part of me feels replaced because Lorelei doesn't shut up about her.

"So, if you're not avoiding the shop teacher, who are you avoiding?"

My eyes widen. Shit. I told Lorelei that my new sub job was exhausting, but it isn't because of the kids. I've been on edge all day at work since Wednesday. I can't relax, and I'm constantly watching the little piece of glass in the door, hoping to catch a glimpse of Chase walking by the room.

I also hope he comes nowhere near me. I've never wanted to see someone and not see someone at the very same time. It's an odd and unsettling feeling. I told Lorelei I was avoiding a great guy at work, and that's when I got the lecture about having low self-esteem. I was hoping she'd still think I was talking about Leo. Where is my brain?

"Is there another guy you're avoiding?" she asks.

I clear my throat and chew on the inside of my cheek like I do when I'm nervous. Unfortunately, Lorelei knows all my tells and puts her hands on her hips. "Spill, Kailee."

I close my eyes and prepare myself. She's going to lose her shit, but I need to talk to someone about this. "Do you remember that night we ran into Liam at the bar and he drove you home?"

"Oh, yeah. I also remember you giving me shit because I let him bend me over the counter and come on my asshole after spanking me with his belt." She squints at me. "What about that night?"

"You know how you left me at the bar with Liam's friend?"

Lorelei stills. Even the oscillating fan passes her face without a single blonde strand of hair moving in the breeze. "Oh, my fucking God! Did something happen with Chase?"

I clasp my hands at the back of my neck and catch my breath. Here it goes. I look away, ashamed. I have no idea why I'm ashamed, though. It could be because I didn't tell my best friend I fucked her man's best friend, or it could be the filthy things I let Chase do to my body. It could be that I enjoyed everything he gave me. "Yeah. Something happened."

"Damn it!" Lorelei yells. Her face reddens until I can hardly see the freckles across her nose.

Looking closer, she's smiling and not angry. "Are you mad or not?" I ask. "I can't tell. You're yelling, but you're grinning like the cat that ate the canary."

"I owe Liam twenty bucks. He suspects something happened, but I said you'd tell me. I'm mad about having to pay up, but I'm totally stoked that something happened with my best friend and the hero I love for saving my Liam."

I squint. "What do you mean that Liam suspected?"

"Oh, he said Chase was all kinds of shifty about the timeline of that night. He changed the subject when Liam flat-out asked if he tapped you."

"Tapped me?"

Lorelei raises her eyebrows. "Did you get tapped while I was bent over the counter?"

I sputter a laugh. "Ironically, I also got bent over the counter. I wasn't just spanked, though. I got fucked into the granite. I stayed over and then panicked in the morning. I left without saying goodbye."

"Well, that explains why he hasn't mentioned it to Liam. Why did you hurt Chase's feelings like that?"

"Wait, wait, wait." I hold up my hand in a stop motion. "We don't know that Chase's feelings were hurt."

"Men are human, Kailee."

"I know they're human," I huff.

"They have feelings, even if they don't always put them into words."

"They also like one-night stands. Anyway, guess who walked into the teacher's lounge on Wednesday? Totally scared the shit out of me. Truth be told, it also made me excited for a few seconds. I thought that maybe, well, maybe he was looking for me to talk. Turns out, he's just filling in as a resource officer. He's a temp like me."

"Liam told me Chase was doing that, but I didn't put two and two together. Let me get this straight. You're working with Chase now. You fucked him nice and dirty, and now you need to work with him and the guy across the hall that wants to date you."

"That's the sum of it. Yes."

"I can't believe you didn't tell me any of this."

"Things were heating up with you and Liam. Chase is Liam's work partner and best friend. I didn't want it to be awkward."

"You need to dump Leo."

I shake my head in surprise like I'm clearing cobwebs from my mind. "What?"

"Don't go out with him."

"Why not? You were just advocating for the guy."

"I need you at the metal concert next weekend."

I push myself off the counter and nail Lorelei with an angry glare. "I know you, Lorelei Rogers," I scold, shaking my finger like she's one of the third graders I regularly sub for. "You're going to tell me you need me for the concert, make me cancel the date with Leo, and a confused Liam will show up to the concert with an even more confused Chase Barnett tagging along. You'll smush us together until we can't avoid each other, and it'll be awkward as fuck. Nope. Not happening."

"Why not?" Lorelei whines. "He's amazing."

"That's the problem."

"Why?" she asks again, louder this time. A partygoer passing the truck startles, grabs a business card, and scurries away.

"I don't know what I'd do with a guy like him long term. I don't do relationships. You know that."

"Times change. We're not nineteen anymore. It's nice to have someone who has an extra set of keys when you lock your keys in the car and can save you from a locksmith charge."

"I'm so happy to hear that your relationship with Liam is so convenient," I chuckle, turning to the counter and grabbing a mixing bowl. "Allow me to drop everything for Chase Barnett and put everything on hold so I have someone to call when I lock my keys in my car. That's kind of why roadside assistance exists."

Lorelei grabs a bottle of vanilla from the cabinet before coming to my side and staring at me. Fuck, she really isn't going to let this go. "It's been six or seven weeks since that night. Can't you set aside any awkwardness from then and give the guy a chance? I could casually set you guys up and..."

Her voice trails off, but I shake my head. "I don't want us pushed together."

Lorelei hums. "But you'd be OK with it if something happened naturally?"

"He's not my type."

"He's what you need, Kailee. Stop running away. Those guys in punk bands won't be there when you're eighty. Let's not talk about the guy with the failed bungee jumping business who disappeared on you after that unfortunate lawsuit. Why can't you admit that Chase is a good choice?"

"I can. He's a great choice, I'm just...well, I'm just scared, OK? There, I said it. I'm scared that it could be real. I'm scared of guys like him. But it's a moot point because he hasn't begged for me back. I haven't even seen him since Wednesday. We're obviously avoiding each other."

"What if he just feels the same way? What if he liked your time together but thinks *you* don't want something?"

I walk to the minifridge and get out a serving of cannabutter that Lorelei premeasures for certain recipes. "Let me make your cookies and leave me be. If it happens, it happens. I don't need you to push us together, and I'll deal with any feelings for Officer Chase Barnett as they arise."

Lorelei holds her hands up and walks to her mixer. "I sincerely hope the universe gives you a swift kick in the ass one of these days, Kailee."

Chapter 6

CHASE

"Hey, man, you coming to the happy hour after work at Frankie's?" Jeff Richter asks, standing in the doorway of the teachers' lounge and looking at my plate of cafeteria food like he's shocked an adult eats it.

I love cafeteria food. It's probably the weirdest thing about me. There's nothing like one of those rectangular school pizzas from back in the day. I'd always eat the cheese first, scrape off the sauce, and then fold the soggy crust over like a taco. Throw in some greasy corn and a scoop of applesauce, and you have the perfect meal.

I stare at Jeff for a moment, thinking. I should go and mingle. My chief is friends with the superintendent of schools and has asked me how it's going here. The only answer I've been able to give my boss is that it's quiet. It's quite the change from my usual drug busts. The only drug issue I've had to handle here isn't even drugs. Kids like to vape in the bathrooms.

I've gone from drug task force cocaine ring busts, undercover investigations, and getting most of my informant information from hookers to walking the halls and sniffing the air for apple-scented vape.

I can't wait until Liam is cleared to work. I still look forward to the coffee selection every day, but I miss my real job. The days I go in for an hour of counseling are the best parts of my week. Just walking through the bullpen and seeing the office staff makes me happy. Temporarily working here is like going to an exotic location for vacation. It's fun for a few days of beach time, but you miss your own bed and routine after too long.

Then again, I'll miss *her*. Not that I've seen her that much, but I do position myself by the upstairs window at arrival time and watch her walk into the building, her lunch box in her hand and a cloth grocery bag over her shoulder. I watch the sway of her hips as she casually glides up the sidewalk, smiling and greeting other teachers. Those same hips that I gripped while I thrust into her tight, little –

"You coming or what? If you're my wingman, you can help me win that bet with Leo. Lipshitz is coming."

I raise my head with renewed interest. I could talk to her outside of work. Would she let me buy her a drink? More importantly, I could piss a circle around her in front of Leo and Jeff and let them know their stupid bet is a pipe dream.

"How do you know?" I ask, mentally praying she hasn't been talking to him. That's one thing I wished we would have done more of – talking. I want to know more about her, especially after watching her walk into work the last few days. She looks so happy and is kind to other people, including her students. That's rare in women I've dated. I don't think I've ever been with a woman who is so willing to look an acquaintance in the eye as she sincerely greets them instead of staring at her phone and giving a curt nod.

Sincere. That's a word I'd use to describe Kailee. Other words would be kind, gorgeous, smart, great with kids, and smells good. If I wait to enter a room until she leaves, I can always smell a hint of her perfume. That's just her perfume, though. That's not the scent I remember from between her legs – the scent that makes my mouth water whenever I think about it.

"Leo asked her," Jeff explains.

Fucking Leo again. This guy needs to fall off a cliff.

I nod and take a bite of corn, trying to remain calm. "Is everyone driving there right after work?"

"Yeah, and we're already at a loss right off the bat."

"Why's that?" I ask.

"Leo's driving Kailee. He'll be working on her the whole way there."

Jeff Richter probably thinks I'm a psycho. I would think someone's a psycho if they squeezed a milk carton with so much force that the custodian has to be called to clean milk off the walls.

***

Frankie's is like being in neon hell. Televisions line the top of the walls, showing soccer and amateur basketball games. Golf is on a big screen in the corner, and men in pleated pants gather around the television like they're watching the Super Bowl. Pink neon signs point the way to the bar and the bathrooms. Blue neon arrows point to the pinball machines in the back of the joint.

When my eyes finally adjust, I head to the bar and order a simple beer. I should stick with one tonight. I sure don't need a drunken repeat of what happened with Kailee the first time we were in a bar together. Not that I'd be opposed to another good roll in my bed. I just want to get to know her more before we go there again. Call me a sap, but this one is girlfriend material, and part of me regrets that we got a few things backward.

"Hey, man," Leo says, sidling up to the bar and slapping me on the back. He must have just got here. The hair on my arms immediately stands at attention. If he's here, she's also in the room. "You coming to sit with us so we can get this humiliation over with?"

I turn and face him, leisurely resting on my elbows and intentionally not looking around the room. I don't want Kailee to think I only came for her by looking for her. "What humiliation is that, Leo?"

He runs his hands over the front of his shirt like he's proud he got to drive her here. Hell, I'd be proud to cart her around, but something tells me Leo feels exceptionally good about it. He doesn't strike me as a ladies' man. The fact that he got to drive her and is showing off to me is so fucking quaint I could cry. It almost hurts the one feeling I have for the guy to have to burst his bubble.

I sip my beer and sigh when he doesn't answer me. "You may have brought her here, but let's take a side bet on who she goes home with."

The smile wipes off his face as the reality of the situation sinks in. He grabs his beer, slides a five-dollar bill across the bar, and sneers as he turns to walk back to the large booth where our coworkers are mingling. "I was just playing. No need to be mean."

"Yeah, bragging about driving her here probably wasn't the best way to get on my good side."

Jeff Richter is an irritating gnat. Leo is a douche, and I don't want him to lay one finger on my girl.

My girl? Where the fuck did that come from?

There she is, sitting elegantly at the table and smiling at one of the female math teachers as the other woman tells her a story. I tilt my head and just watch her while I sip my beer. I could stand here all night. I won't though – not with Leo's arm slung over the back of the booth behind her like he owns her. He smirks at me when he gets settled, and he makes a pointing motion above Kailee's head, indicating to Jeff that he's sitting next to her. Jeff good-naturedly shakes his head and shrugs, apparently accepting defeat.

I'll never surrender her to the douchey shop teacher.

"Hi, Kailee," I say, sliding into the booth next to her. Leo is on her other side, and Kailee's eyes momentarily widen like she's stuck between a rock and a hard place. "How was your week?"

My words are clipped and short. I smile to reassure her that I'm not pissed at her. She probably thinks I'm a jealous monster right now. As I wait for her answer, I run my eyes over as much of her body as I can without seeming pervy. She's in a cream sweater with wide holes on both shoulders, black jeans, and black heeled boots I'd like to peel off one at a time before pulling her naughty little panties down.

And that smell. *Her* smell.

"Fine, Chase. How was your week?"

I lean forward and whisper in her ear, intentionally grazing her jaw with my cheek. "I thought you should know that the guy next to you started a bet with Jeff about who can get your panties off fastest."

Kailee blinks and silently looks at the table for a few moments as she grits her teeth. Her fingers grip the hem of her sweater and she turns so our noses almost bump. Her breath smells like peppermint gum. "What?"

"The guy has a major crush on you."

"I know that," she whispers so Leo can't hear. "He asked me out."

I run a finger up her leg under the table. She startles a little but her eyes momentarily flutter before she controls herself. "Are you going to go out with him? Because honestly, I'd like to take you out."

I'm suddenly pushed roughly out of the booth as she grabs the glass of wine in front of her and pushes me out of the seat. "Move. Back there," she says, pointing at the pink neon above the bathroom.

"What? Why?" I ask, confused.

"We need to have a chat," she hisses, her teeth clenched.

Behind her, Leo frowns like he doesn't like me getting any alone time with her. Fuck that dickhead. He got to drive her here. I turn and let her frog march me to the back of the bar, and I hold my hands up like her hand on my back is a gun. "Careful, Pussycat. People may think you're taking me back here for a quick shag." I smile at my own joke. "And I can make that happen if you ask nicely."

We enter the bright bathroom hallway, and she spins me to face her. "Number one, there will be no more shagging. Number two, don't call me Pussycat. Nicknames are my thing. Number three, what the fuck are you talking about with a bet?"

"Just what I said. Jeff came to me on the first day and told me that he and Leo have a bet about getting in your panties," I say, leaning my arm on the wall and propping my head on it. I hope I look sexy. "I didn't have the heart to tell them I've already won that bet." Her face reddens, and I squint in confusion. "Why are you so mad at me? I'm telling you about it so you know."

She inhales sharply. "Chase, did you take the bet too?"

"No. I didn't need to. I already won." She scowls at me. Backpedal. Backpedal. Abort. Abort. "I just told you so you'd know and could be safe."

"This is the most immature bullshit I've heard from adult males. Have you all been sniffing the art room glue?"

"I haven't done that since my own high school days."

She shakes her head a moment. "I've seen better maturity from my high school classes. Hell, this is something that happens when I sub fifth grade. What the fuck is wrong with you people?"

"Go out with me." The words just pop out, mostly because I have no idea how to defend myself now that I've heard someone say how immature their bet is, and I'm immature for telling her. "Seriously, Kailee. We had a great time when we were together, but let's go out for dinner and actually get to know each other."

"You want to get to know me?"

I step closer to her. If I lean down just a little, I could kiss her. Memories of those warm lips on mine fill my mind, and my heart pounds in my chest. "Have dinner with me. One dinner. No sex on the counter. No face riding. I mean, that was fun, but let me get to know the cowgirl inside," I say, pointing to her heart. She rolls her eyes. "If nothing else, we can clear the air since we'll be around each other more with Lorelei and Liam dragging us places together. Let's at least be friends, Kailee."

Friends, my ass. I swear to fucking God, if this beautiful creature puts me in the friend zone, I'll scream into a pillow. Dear Christ, don't let me have to see her hold hands with the fucking shop teacher.

She puts her hands on her hips and taps her foot. "Thanks for telling me, but I'm a big girl and can handle my own shit."

"So you won't go out with Leo?"

She smiles an evil grin that would be at home in a horror movie. "Like I said, Chase. I'm a big girl and make my own decisions. He asked nicely."

Chapter 7

KAILEE

"What do you do for fun?" Leo asks. I can't drink my wine fast enough for this date.

"I worship Satan."

Leo laughs and continues picking loose skin off one of his fingers. He's been doing it all night. A nervous habit?

Why am I even here? Oh, I know. It's because bachelor number one, Leo, made a bet with bachelor number two, Jeff, and bachelor number three, Chase, told me about it to butter me up for his own purposes. I should go out with all of them and deny all three so they can cry about it together.

Honestly, I'll have a hard time turning down Chase. The man makes my toes curl just by looking at him. I find myself looking for him and hoping he'll pop into the teacher's lounge when I'm there. OK, I *may* give that one a chance.

In the meantime, I have to survive the date with bachelor number one, when all I want to do is scratch my eyes out at the walking boredom that is Leo. So far, I've heard about his Voltron model collection, how his last two dates didn't match their listed weights on Tinder, and his disc golf record score.

"Do you like car shows?" he asks, glossing over the Satanic worship tidbit.

"Not really."

He smiles. Jesus fucking Christ, what is it with guys? The bigger of a bitch you are, the more they fawn over you.

My stomach clenches, and I eye the salad in front of me with disdain. It's a normal-looking salad with lettuce, tomatoes, onions, cucumber, and croutons with a side of ranch dressing. I usually love salads just like it, but my stomach roars as I mix the ranch with the vegetables. I'll just shut up and eat my salad so I can go home, use my vibrator while I think about bachelor number three yet again, and go about my life tomorrow.

"I listen to bluegrass records. What kind of music do you like?" Leo asks.

It's a nice question. For any other woman in the world, except for his last two dates who were obviously judged by their respective weights, Leo Paulson is a catch. Just not for me.

"I listen to punk," I say, swallowing the last word because something else wants to come out of my mouth.

I must pale or turn green because Leo leans over his own salad and grabs my hand. "Are you OK?"

His hand is so hot that it burns me, and I pull away. I reach for my water glass and down it in three gulps, only to be rewarded with more fuss from my stomach. Whatever's happening in there, the water is making it worse.

"Excuse me. I need to go to the restroom."

I don't wait for a response or worry about how he feels. I break into a sprint for the bathroom and almost take out our waitress as she rounds the corner from the kitchen with a plate of what I assume is my steak and baked potato.

I quickly search for the restroom, scanning left and right. Eventually, I ask the bartender, who instinctively backs away from me as he points. I'm green around the gills. I feel it.

I barely make it to the toilet. In fact, a little gets on the floor in front of the bowl as everything comes up. Salad. Wine. Half my lunch. I'm pretty sure I see the scrambled eggs from breakfast, too. What the hell? Is there a stomach flu that I got from the students?

The door creaks open, and a pair of work boots approaches my cubicle. "Kailee?" Leo asks in a kind voice. Why can't I like him?

Oh yeah…He judges women by their weight, is boring as hell, and he's not Chase fucking Barnett.

"I'm OK. I'll just be a minute."

"You don't sound OK, and you looked terrible right before you ran for it. Can I get you anything? A wet rag?"

Hot, brown vomit comes out of me, and my stomach muscles squeeze so hard that I momentarily worry I may have to change my pants. I haven't thrown up like this in years. I threw up about three weeks ago from some bad fish or something, but this is violent.

Food poisoning?

"Can you call my friend? Her name is Lorelei. She's in my contacts. Ask her if she can come get me." I slide my clutch purse under the stall to Leo, not even caring that I'll have to disinfect it later because it touched the gross floor. I don't want anyone to see me like this, but if someone has to see me, Lorelei is the only option.

Leo silently picks up my purse and ruffles through my bag. There's nothing interesting in there except my wallet, phone, and keys, so I have nothing to worry about. It's not like he'll find a condom I was hoping to use tonight.

I intentionally didn't pack one because I knew I wouldn't sleep with him.

I hear my phone connect the call, and I breathe out a sigh of relief. Please pick up, Lorelei.

***

"Damn, girl, how much did you drink?" Lorelei asks, holding a cold cloth to my neck. Always have a friend who will pick you up from a restaurant, hold a popcorn bucket in front of you as she walks you out the back door, and hold your hair while you throw up when you get home.

"Just one glass of wine."

"What did you eat?"

"A few bites of salad. Do you think it had bacteria on it or something?"

"I don't think it would have hit you this fast. That usually takes some time to set in. What did you have yesterday?" She asks, handing me a paper towel to wipe my face.

"Soup and watermelon. I didn't feel like eating much, and when I ate the soup, I got so hot that I ate the watermelon. It's all I wanted."

Lorelei crinkles her eyes and sits back from me on her heels. She runs her hands down her jean-clad thighs and then pulls her own strawberry-blonde hair back into a ponytail with a sigh. "I'm going to ask you a question, and I don't want you to be offended. I just want you to think about it, OK?"

I nod and move my head back over the toilet. I feel like I'm going to puke again.

"When was your last period?"

"Why would you even ask that?"

Lorelei ignores me. "When was your last period?"

I lift my head a little and grab the glass of water on the counter as I think. "I don't know. I've never been regular. A couple months ago or something? I'm sure I'll get it soon. I go three months in between sometimes, and then it's heavy and excruciating. It's been that way since my first period at eleven. It comes when it wants to."

Lorelei looks at me without blinking. "Kailee, are you pregnant?"

The world spins, and I'm not sure if it's sickness or shock. It's a good thing my head is already over the toilet, and I set my face on the toilet rim. The plastic of the seat is cool, and I could stay here forever. I'll just sit here and think while my face is parked somewhere it can't cause a mess. Lorelei reaches out and pats my back.

Could I be pregnant? I've always had a messed-up cycle, even suffering from endometriosis so much that my doctor told me years ago that I may have trouble conceiving. I've had ablations, and I had surgery that left uterine scars, severely reducing my fertility. That's what I was told anyway. It was in the damn brochure and on the form I signed before I had the surgery which was the last-ditch effort before a hysterectomy. If I'm pregnant, I'll write a strongly worded letter to that idiot doctor.

I mentally tick off any other signs I've had lately. I've been tired. So tired that I've wanted to die just so I could get some sleep. I thought it was a lack of sunlight in the cooking dungeon that was making me tired all day at work. I can hardly drag myself out of bed in the morning. My boobs hurt, but I thought it was because I got a few new bras and the fit was wrong. I'm hot. So hot all the time. I actually thought I might be in early menopause last week while working on the truck. Nobody else seems bothered by heat, but I want to stick my face in a refrigerator when it hits me. I wouldn't put it past my body to go through early menopause with all the issues I've had, so I thought nothing of it.

My chest clenches, and something visceral happens in my abdomen. Nerves. No – this is fear. Terror. "Oh, my fucking God. What the fuck am I going to do?"

"I'm going to go get a test at the drugstore up the street," Lorelei says, getting off the floor. "I'll be back in ten minutes. Will you be OK?"

"I'm going to be sick."

"You're already sick," Lorelei says as she walks out of my bathroom. "I'll be right back."

My front door slams shut, and a tear dribbles down my face. This can't be happening. Tired. Sick. Boob hurt. All of it blends together in my mind. My cycle is always off, so I don't blame myself that I missed this, but there's so much more to this than being tired and sick.

Living paycheck to paycheck. Government insurance. Single. I have a one-bedroom apartment, for fuck's sake. Does the government require the baby to have a separate room? Why hasn't anyone told me any of these things? Do the police come to check to make sure you have a crib for them?

The police.

Chase.

Oh. My. Fucking. God.

A guttural sound comes from my throat. I haven't been with anyone since our one-night stand, and I hadn't had sex in months before Chase. I haven't talked to my mother in three years, but I can practically hear her chastise me for creating another human being with a total stranger while bent over a kitchen counter.

I swear to God, I really didn't think I could get pregnant with all my past issues. I was told by a medical professional that it was unlikely. I always use condoms. What is the chance that a woman who was told she may never be able to conceive gets pregnant the single time she has one too many margaritas and doesn't tell the dude to glove up?

Chase Barnett's new nickname should be Officer Super Sperm.

Lorelei is back within minutes and breezes back into the room, a frown lining her face. She usually smiles around me, but her entire demeanor is off. She understands the seriousness of this. She probably thinks I couldn't mother my way out of a paper bag. I wish she'd smile or crack a fetus joke. Something.

"I'm going to give you some privacy. Can you pee?" she asks.

"I think I can work some up," I say, letting her help me off the floor.

As soon as she leaves the bathroom and shuts my pocket sliding door, I undo my pants and quickly sit on the toilet. I pee as fast as I can, making sure I hit the tester stick, and throw the stick on the counter before squatting in front of the toilet again. "I'm done. You can come in."

Lorelei comes back into the room and glances at the stick while standing safely at the door. "Did you look?"

I shake my head. "I can't. You do it. If I do it, it makes it real."

"It's real anyway if there are two lines there, Kailee."

Something on my face must tell her I'm not capable of this, and she creeps closer to the counter, craning her neck to look at the test. When she reads it, she picks it up and squints.

"Just tell me."

She looks at me, a sad look on her face, and I know what she's going to say before she says it. My face crinkles, and I throw up again. This time, I'm not sure if it's from being sick or the scary realization that I'm someone's mother now.

Lorelei is at my side in a moment, her arm around me. "It's OK, Kailee. We'll get through this. Take a couple days and decide what you want to do, but since you're probably already several weeks along, we'll need to decide fast."

"How many weeks do you think?"

She shrugs, "It depends on when you got pregnant. Pregnancy weeks are counted from the first day of a last period," she explains. "Women are already four weeks by the time they miss a period. Women like you, with irregular cycles, are often surprised by the time they get to seven or eight."

I nod. "I can't have this baby, Lorelei. I can't. What kind of mother would I be?"

"You'd be a great one. That's not even a problem here."

"Are you insane? Look at my life." I raise my arm and half-ass gesture toward my bedroom. "I don't even make my bed. Aren't moms supposed to make their beds?"

"I see a woman who works two jobs and is educated enough to work one if she wants to tie herself down. I'm not saying things wouldn't have to change, but you've got this. What about help from the father?"

The fact that Lorelei doesn't assume Chase is the father strikes me as funny. Sure, I've been known to date a couple of guys at a time, but I'm offended Lorelei thinks there are a lot of options for me to choose from. What's next? Asking me to parade a bunch of men on a talk show to take DNA tests?

"He's not involved."

She clears her throat. "Do you know who it is?"

I slap my hand against the toilet tank in frustration. "What kind of question is that of your best friend? Of course, I know who it is."

I put my face back in the toilet and let the tears fall on the gross water below.

"Who's the father?" she whispers.

"Chase."

Lorelei blows out a sigh and is silent for a few moments. When she does make a sound, it's an odd hum before she speaks. "Holy fucking shit! I didn't want to assume, but... Kailee! What the fuck?"

I lift my head, and my vision swirls. It's been a rough night, and I just want to crawl into bed and never get out again. "You can't say anything."

"How can I not say anything? It's Chase's baby!"

"Just give me a few days to work out what I'm going to do. I don't know what'll happen. I'm making this up as I go along, and I've had about three minutes to even think about it. I'm not exactly sane right now."

"I cannot keep this from Liam, and he probably can't keep it from Chase."

"Please, Lorelei." I hear the pleading in my voice, and I'm ashamed. "You can't tell Liam because I need to tell Chase myself. Wouldn't you want to be the one to tell Liam you were pregnant?" My body heaves with another sob as I wipe the snot away from my nose.

She bites her lip before quietly going into my adjoining bedroom and pulling my blanket off my bed. She drapes it around me and tucks it around my waist. The gesture is so maternal. I wish I could take this...thing and give it to her. She'd be much better at it.

She refills my water glass and flushes the toilet for me like I'm a child. "Fine," she finally says. "But I know you, Kailee. You have to tell him. No pulling this thing where you avoid him and he never finds out, or he finds out twenty years from now when his kid shows up at his door."

Chapter 8

CHASE

I know she's in there, so I saunter into the teacher's lounge with the panther-like walk I reserve for approaching women at bars. Thankfully, she sits by herself at a table near the vending machine, and I take a moment to check her out as the door shuts with a click behind me. I imagine she's seeing me in all my glory by the door as I smile at her, but she doesn't look thrilled.

In fact, she looks downright miserable. Tired.

Her hair is in a messy bun again, but strands hang down wildly like she didn't brush her hair before she put it up today. Her normally pink skin is pale, and dark circles line her undereye area like she didn't get a wink of sleep last night.

My face scrunches in concern, and I step toward her, forgetting to look cool or impress her. Fuck that shit. It's more important that she's OK with whatever's going on.

"Kailee? Are you OK?" I ask. I pull a chair out and immediately sit without invitation. "Did someone die?"

"Only my future," she mumbles and looks back to her Tupperware dish containing a clear broth.

"What do you mean? Did something happen with your job?"

She snorts a laugh and wipes her nose. "No, Chase." She taps the spoon on the side of her container and reaches for a nearby roll. Plain. No butter. "I just haven't been feeling well lately."

"I hope you don't have that stomach issue that hit the junior class."

She stares at me for a few seconds. "I sure hope the juniors don't have this."

"Can I do anything to help?" I ask.

Her eyes widen and she looks down at her soup. "Oh, I think I'll need your help at some point, but I'm just...not ready to talk yet, OK?" She practically whispers the words. "And not here."

I straighten in my seat and smile. She'll need my help. I love being the hero. Hell, I probably have a hero complex. Many police officers do, and it's often why we go into law enforcement. I want to be *her* hero. I want to be needed by her. Sure, I don't know Kailee well, but I want to know her better with all my being. There's just something about her I still can't pinpoint that makes me want to pull her to my chest and never let her go. It could be that she's so independent and does her own thing. It could be because I see something under that - something crying out to have someone to lean on in hard times.

Someone hurt her once, and I want to lick her wounds...everywhere.

She said she'd let me help her. Not Leo. Not Jeff. She didn't even mention Liam, who I thought would be first on the list now that he's dating Kailee's best friend.

Before I can think more about it, she looks up at me with tears in her eyes. Her nose reddens, and my smile leaves my face. I reach for her hand resting near her soup bowl, and she allows me to run my thumb over her skin. I watch her face, silently pleading for her to talk to me. Tell me what's wrong.

"Hi, Kailee," a deep voice says, interrupting my thoughts and making Kailee jump.

Leo stomps to the table and sets his lunch box down as Kailee pulls her hand out from under mine. I miss her warmth. I miss her skin next to mine. I could positively kill Leo Paulson because I'm fairly certain Kailee was about to spill her guts.

I know she felt the spark when our skin touched. I almost had her.

Leo also noticed. "What's going on here?" he asks, sniffing. "You two dating now?"

"No," Kailee says in a clipped tone, and my heart sinks. Was she offended he even thought that? "Just friends talking. I'm having a rough day."

Leo slides into the seat next to mine, and it's all I can do not to roll my eyes as he opens up his lunch box and pulls out two gigantic sub sandwiches and three cheese sticks. Kailee also looks away. Maybe she doesn't like cheese sticks.

"So, what's new, Barnett?" Leo asks. He eyes the hand that was just on top of Kailee's, and I think hard about curling it into a fist and hitting him in the face. He looks at Kailee and jerks his chin at her. "If you're not dating this guy, can I get a rain check on our date last night?"

Date last night? Rain check? Something stirs in my stomach, and it takes me a second to recognize the feeling of hope. I *hope* she ran out through the back kitchen.

My eyes flick to Kailee's face, and I force my facial muscles into a neutral expression. I can't show the rage or jealousy I feel. She looks away from me.

"I don't know, Leo. Right now, I just need to deal with not feeling great."

"Yeah, I'm surprised to see you here the way you were tossing your cookies in the restaurant bathroom."

At least she wasn't making up not feeling well. I guess she's really sick, but I still don't like the idea that she was on a date with the tool next to me.

I take deep breaths through my nose, trying to avoid losing my temper. Every fiber of my being tells me to stomp and stew like a toddler throwing a temper tantrum. Why him? Why did he get to take her out, and she won't let me go out with her? I thought she was fucking with me when she said she was going out with him because he asked nicely. I'm way better for her than this guy, and I have an equally great public pension.

"Thanks for calling Lorelei for me," Kailee says.

Color me confused. She had Leo call Lorelei when she was sick?

Something's going on.

"Is there anything you need?" I ask. "I'm going to the store on my break next hour." I really wasn't planning on it, but it just slipped out of my mouth. I want to do something for her and actively help.

Leo side eyes me. "Yeah, I have planning period. I can get you some Tums or something."

"Ginger ale is better," I say, nailing Leo with a glare. Thank fuck I paid attention to how Liam helped his mother through chemo.

"I have some saltines in my drawer," Leo counters.

"I may have Pepto in my glove compartment."

"I can make you some toast. Someone left bread," Leo says, gesturing to the cabinets behind us.

"Instead of feeding you old bread, Kailee, I'll walk down the street to Panera and get you some chicken soup."

Leo and I both practically pant and stare at each other as we one-up each other on nausea remedies. My lip curls, and his twitches. Fear maybe? Knowing I'm better looking and just as willing to do whatever she needs?

I drop the mic. The nail in the coffin. I draw out the words as I look at Leo, our noses practically touching, neither of us blinking. "I can get you...Jell-O."

Leo backs away, his lips in a pale, straight line, and Kailee gasps. "Chase, I can't ask you to take time out of your day to do that for me."

I finally break Leo's glare and turn to face Kailee again. "Nothing, and I mean nothing, would give me as much pleasure as procuring Jell-O for you, baby."

When I call her baby, Kailee doesn't bat an eye, but something in Leo panics. His eyes widen, and his nostrils flare. He squeezes one of the sub sandwiches so hard that the meat and bread squish together until they're goo. His face reddens until I'm worried he's having a heart attack. But he's a formidable opponent. Even I can see that.

He refuses to quit. "Want me to come over and make dinner for you tonight, Kailee?" he asks. "We didn't get through it last night."

Now it's my turn to fume. Absolutely fucking not. I can't abide this douche in her home, cooking and doing all the things I want to do for her. "I'm sure she's not up for that if she's sick, bro."

"Yeah, Leo. That's really nice of you, but I think I'm just going to take it easy and sit around tonight. Maybe watch some Netflix."

"Ok, no food then." Jesus, this guy doesn't give up. I almost respect it. "I'll come over and watch TV with you."

Kailee looks down and stirs what's left of her soup. "Thanks, Leo, but I'm just not in the mood."

She turned him down! She doesn't want him. How many times have I been told that if a woman is really interested in a man, she'll crawl over a bed of hot coals to spend time with him? It works both ways, and I can honestly say I'd crawl over a bed of hot coals to bring this woman Jell-O later. Hell, if I was sick with Ebola, I'd put on a hazmat suit if she wanted me to make her dinner.

Eat shit, Leo!

The bell that ends Kailee's lunch period rings, and she quickly gets up from her seat, hazarding a glance at Leo and me. Is she worried we'll box for her honor as soon as she leaves?

Shaking her head, she eventually throws her napkin away and walks to the door.

"Kailee?" I ask.

She turns around and straightens her shoulders. "Yes, Chase?"

"What flavor do you want?"

She smiles, and I see the chance I really have. There's something in the smile that tells me she's at least open to the idea of giving me a chance. Her face relaxes, and her mouth opens like she's ready to read a monologue. I can tell there's so much she wants to let out.

After a few moments, she closes her mouth and clears her throat. "Anything red," she says before walking out the door and not saying another word to Leo.

As soon as the smell of her perfume follows her out the door, Leo whirls on me, his face red. Hell, his neck and ears are bright red. This guy is a heart attack waiting to happen.

"Why'd you do that?" he asks.

"Why'd I do what? Help my friend and offer to get her Jell-O?" I stand and put my hands in my pockets. "Newsflash, bro, you don't own her." I lean forward so that I'm looking down at him. He backs away in surprise that I'm willing to get that close. "In fact, I've known her since before I worked here."

"What? You know Kailee?"

"Her best friend dates my best friend." I straighten and watch Leo's face fall. He knows. He knows that if our friends want us to get together, they'll push for it, and that will give me an edge.

"Here's what's going to happen," I say. I stick my index finger in his face, and his eyes cross as he looks at it. "I'm going to go get her the Jell-O I promised, and you're going to get the fuck out of my way when it comes to her."

I arrogantly cross my arms the way I do with drug suspects who know they're fucked.

But Leo Paulson, shop teacher extraordinaire, is no cornered drug dealer. "No," he says, shaking his head. He opens his cheese stick and takes a big bite of it without peeling the strings. Fuck, I can't stand when people eat them that way. "I think I'll keep asking until she tells me outright that I'm not wanted. Let her make the decision."

Hm. Interesting concept. "I can get behind that. But if she chooses one of us, the other backs off."

It's going to be me, loser.

He nods. "Fine, but you'll just break her heart anyway."

I jolt back. "Excuse the fuck out of me?"

He idly waves his hand at standard resource officer getup of a department shirt, black pants, and weapons on my belt. He nods toward the gun at my waist. "You're a cop. Cops have hard relationships. Everyone knows that. Things can also happen to you."

Heat rushes to my toes, and I momentarily worry my blood is literally boiling because he's not wrong. How many divorces have I seen on the force because guys like me go home to their wives and can't talk about the downright cesspool of shit they see on a daily basis? How many girlfriends say that the risk of getting the phone call we've been shot is too great of a worry? Hell, Liam almost died a few weeks ago. I never thought I'd be in the same situation because my dating life is a revolving door, but would the woman I ultimately want pass me over for a mediocre man with a sensible job because what I do isn't safe?

Then again, Leo works around teenagers with access to power tools. I'll take the drug dealers.

"We'll see what Kailee decides," I say, trying to control my voice. I can't let him think he's getting to me.

"You're a ladies' man. Forget about her and let me have a shot. You'll find someone else."

Fuck no.

I lean down again and grit my teeth. "I. Want. Her."

There are no flipping opinions on it anymore. There's no worry that our one-night stand was backwards and I should just let her go. I want her down to my core. My balls tighten at the idea of losing her. It's a visceral response, and it sets my blood on fire. I want to protect her, love her, and make whatever is bothering her fuck off into the wind.

He shrugs like he couldn't give a shit that I want her, but I know he does. His shoulders heave with the energy it takes not to get out of the chair and take a swing at me. My job is to know when someone is going to attack or at least wants to hurt me. I'm trained for it, and I see it in his eyes.

The fifth-period bell rings, and it's time for me to walk around the last lunch period of the day. Leo and I both reflexively look at the clock on the wall.

"Maybe you shouldn't make bets over women. She's a human being. You and Jeff are toddlers. If you'll excuse me, I have to do a walk-through and then procure some red Jell-O for a beautiful woman." I pat him on the shoulder as I walk toward the door. "I'll wave at you through your window when I take it to her."

Chapter 9

KAILEE

The waiter sets down the saltines I requested, and Lorelei shakes her head. "Still not feeling well?"

I reach for the packets and ignore the salad in front of me that sounded good at the time. "I want to die. I want to positively die. In fact, I may just faceplant right here in this salad. Has anyone ever passed away from this?"

"Pregnancy or morning sickness?" Lorelei asks, biting her lip. "Because with pregnancy, the United States has one of the worst maternal death rates of all developed countries. Morning sickness? I'm not so sure about the death rate, but I remember reading of a few celebrities that had it terribly."

I roll my shoulders and glare at my best friend. "Thanks for the info on my impending death. While I wait for the end, maybe I'll call my buddies in the Hollywood realm and get some puke tips."

Lorelei's normally pink cheeks turn a beet red, and she frowns. "Yeah, I probably shouldn't have told you about the death thing. That's not helpful."

I shut my menu with a huff and jam a saltine in my mouth. "Fuck! This is horrible."

Lorelei smiles at the waiter when he comes to take our order, and she orders salmon with rice pilaf. When she mentions the salmon, I turn my head and cover my mouth with a napkin while angling for the nearby empty wine bucket by the table in case I need it. Thankfully, I don't.

"For you, ma'am?" the waiter asks, totally oblivious to my plight.

"Do you have chicken broth?"

His eyes crease together. "We have a chicken noodle soup as our soup of the day. It's that or potato cheese."

"Can you strain the noodles out?"

He frowns. "You want me to strain the noodles out of our chicken noodle soup?"

"And the chicken," I say, nodding.

He writes on his pad, probably something like *strain the chicken for the nutso at table 5,* and walks away, flipping his pad shut like I just asked him to make me a peanut butter and jelly sandwich. Actually, that sounds good, and I raise my finger to get his attention. Unfortunately, he walks back to the kitchen and doesn't see.

"Have you told him?" Lorelei asks in a whisper.

"I just did. I said to strain the noodles and the chicken."

Lorelei blows out a breath so hard that it moves the wisps of hair around her face. "Chase, Kailee. Did you tell Chase you're pregnant?"

I slump in my seat like I'm a five-year-old being chastised for bad table manners. "I couldn't."

"What do you mean you couldn't?"

"I tried!" I practically yell. A couple nearby looks over and raises their eyebrows. Lorelei gives a slight wave. "I opened my mouth to tell him yesterday and almost barfed on him. It was all that was going to come out. Then, Leo came into the lounge."

"Fuck Leo. When Chase asks why you barfed, you just tell him. You just look up at him and say, 'Chase, I'm pregnant with your kitchen counter child.' He'll hug you, and you fall into his arms. Knowing Chase, he'll fuss over you and protect you forever and ever." She puts her hands over her chest, positively gushing about her boyfriend's best friend. She only feels that way because Chase saved her beloved's life.

"Is that what you think will happen? I'm pretty sure it only works like that in books or movies. That's not real life."

Lorelei leans forward and drops her voice. "Have you decided what you're going to do? Are you having it?"

I shrug and look around the restaurant, blinking back tears. I really don't want to cry in front of her. "I don't know. I'm fifty-fifty now. There are moments when I think I could make this work, even if Chase doesn't want to be involved."

"He'd be involved. He'd stand by you and pay child support, even if you two don't work out. I know he would. He'd be involved and help with the baby." There's Lorelei with the hero worship again. God, why doesn't she just marry Liam *and* Chase?

"That's great, but just because a guy wants to be involved doesn't mean it'd be easy for anyone. I've gone over my bank statements, and nothing makes sense."

"Move in with him. He has a nice house with more than one bedroom."

I lean forward and drop my voice to her level. "I haven't told him yet. You don't know he'd just swing the door open and let me move in. There's also the impact on my body. It just feels wrong, you know?"

"You're sick. It happens, but it'll be better further along."

"I also don't want to regret anything if I get an abortion. But right now...I don't think I would. Regret it, I mean. I'm scared. My body hurts and rejects everything I eat, and this is the easy part. My mother had complications having me, nearly dying, and I'm scared of an emergency cesarean like she had. I live alone. I have no partner to help me recover. These are all real problems real women deal with in this situation, and I wish you'd stop making it out as being some fairy-tale ending for me."

Lorelei nods. She can't wait to have children. She's always talked about it. We've also talked about how I'm ambivalent to the idea, mostly because I didn't think I *could* have kids. I just thought, if I ever did magically get pregnant, it'd be after I've been married to a guy for five years, owned a sprawling house, and had more than eighty-five dollars in the bank. I thought I'd need fertility intervention if I ever really wanted a baby. I also said I'd be fine adopting a foster child or something someday. Childbirth scares me, my own mother not having the hip span for it. I'm built like her. She was strongly advised not to have more after me, and she didn't. I left an impression on her.

"What about help from some of those organizations that are always going on about keeping babies..." Her voice trails off and she leans forward.

I bite my lip, trying not to burst out laughing. "Ah, yes. I'm sure the meal train, a few packs of diapers, and a few prayers will do wonders for me. Then, they'll skip off, congratulating themselves for their two hours of counseling and a plastic donation bag full of their benevolence. Come on, Lorelei, you and I discussed it a couple years ago when the shit went down.

"They want babies to get here, and then mothers are on their own, left without money for diapers, formula, and childcare while she works, while everyone who wants the baby born so badly slinks off after clapping for themselves and donating a few bottles of formula. Hell, those same people scream about wanting food stamps and other benefits for mothers cut, and if I have this baby, I'll need the WIC. I'll need the government medical exchange they want to cut. I'll need the daycare subsidies while they'll tar and feather me for being a working mother or denigrate me for wanting the subsidies if I *do* work. They'll taunt me for not working if I can't afford to, calling me lazy and a welfare case. I'll need a lot more than a few meals, diapers, and directions to a food bank. They call us lazy for asking for help, then turn around with fake smiles and ask us why we didn't ask them for help. We're supposed to swoon over donated baby clothes the child will grow out of in weeks. Are they going to clothe my child all its life? Feed it forever? Where is the help for women like me? Women who are scared and broke? For fuck's sake, where is the help for the *children* in this? The same people want to cut free lunch for grade school children. What the actual fuck?

"I don't want to hear another word about their bullshit until the day comes that they actually do something more tangible to help mothers and children in crisis and actually push for policy that helps single mothers and doesn't hurt them. There's no help for women like me. Not real help, anyway. I don't give a flying fuck what they think until they stop smiling at women like me out of one side of the mouth while advocating and voting to cut all the things that will actually help me out of the other side."

"Adoption?" Lorelei asks.

"You sound just like them. That doesn't help with complications. A woman's body still has to go through some hard shit. Pregnancy. Labor. Recovery. All of that was hard for my own mother, and with my medical history may be hard for me. And where the fuck is the mental health and emotional support for those mothers that give up a child only because they're poor? That's some fucked up shit, Lorelei. If they really cared one iota about babies, they'd help women who wouldn't normally give their babies up if they had money. They'd support preschool, daycare, and food benefits for the children that are already here." I wave my hands in front of my face and take a drink of my water. "I'll have to go to Illinois if I get an abortion. That means time off work and losing at least a day's pay. Maybe more. If I take the pill set, it would be better, but I just haven't researched it."

I put my head in my hands and lean over my place setting, blinking back tears. "I can't keep a single thought in my head. It's all over the place. Who do I call for help? What do I do? What do I even Google? I try researching what to do, Lorelei, but my hands shake so bad as I type the words. I feel like I'm losing my mind and in panic mode."

Lorelei straightens and pastes a smile on her face as the waiter puts our plates down in front of us. I intentionally don't look at Lorelei's fish, and I pick up my sad bowl of chicken broth and sip it, grimacing at the bland taste. That peanut butter and jelly sounds better and better. In fact, I lick my lips at the thought of it. If someone handed me a plate of expensive steak and a plate of peanut butter and jelly, I'd choose the latter right now.

"You're being stubborn not telling him," Lorelei says as soon as the waiter leaves. "He's the father. Also, he can help. He can help financially if you choose to have it. If you don't, he could also help with maybe paying for the abortion pills or any wages you miss. Maybe both and any travel expenses. He won't leave your ass out in the wind like some men do. I know you're scared, but he's a good guy, which is more than a lot of the women you mentioned have. So many women are alone in this. Alone and scared."

"I'm scared. I'm scared shitless." I tap my spoon on the bowl and blink to hold back tears. "And I'm pissed off, Lorelei. For every reason I just said. I know I'm not the only woman in the world dealing with this, and the world has made this decision harder for women. You'd think they wouldn't want birth control to go away, but a lot of them do. Not all, but enough to count. You'd think we'd have the best medical care in the world so I wouldn't be terrified of paying an outrageous hospital bill that's more than my annual salary, but we don't. You'd think we'd have paid maternity leave so women can establish breastfeeding and bond with their child, but we don't. As you mentioned, many men, some married and cheating on their wives in the first place, are the first to run away or even take their mistress to another state for an abortion while voting to take away my right to get it up the street in the next election cycle. If there's one thing I can't stand, it's hypocrisy, and those people are full of fantasy world shit while completely lacking empathy for anyone in my situation. They don't empathize because they need to feel superior or like they're saving the world. In reality, they're damning a woman or even girl to possible medical issues, birth trauma, postpartum issues, and possible lifetime poverty. No fucking thank you."

I stir the broth and drop my voice. It's not her fault. I'm not telling her anything she doesn't already know. "I know I need to tell him. It's just hard, you know? I'll get to it."

I'm breathing hard by now, but she lets me vent – knows I need this.

"You need to spend more time with him before you decide anything. It'll also give you a way to feel him out a bit."

"Do you want me to ask how many kids he wants on the first date before I barf in his lasagna?"

"Yes."

***

Lorelei drops me off, and I slink up the stairs to my apartment. Stairs. Fuck, if I have a c-section, I can't even get into my apartment unless I pay Mr. Michelson, the apartment maintenance guy, to carry me up the stairs. What am I going to do? Get piggyback rides?

Would Chase carry me up the stairs? Would he let me stay at his house if I have to have a surgical procedure that renders me incapable of climbing stairs, driving, or lifting anything heavier than my baby?

Something tells me he would.

I couldn't tell him at school today. This isn't a bomb you suddenly drop on someone at their place of work. I need to ease into this. In fact, I don't know if I'll tell him right away. I'm still wrapping my head around it. I'd like to tell him when I have a clear plan.

But Lorelei is right about one thing. I need to talk to him and establish a friendship, at the very least, with him. No more giving him a hard time. No more going out with Leo to make him jealous. The game has drastically changed, even if he doesn't know it yet.

Once inside my apartment, I slide my phone out of my pocket and punch in the numbers Lorelei gave me.

Text to Chase: Hi. It's Kailee. I got your number from Lorelei. Can we talk?

Dots.

More dots.

I glance at the stove clock, and dots have shown on my phone for a full four minutes. Is he writing his entire life story?

I expect something along the lines of, "I was born in a small town by a river" when my phone finally dings with an incoming message.

Text from Chase: Sure.

Either he's the slowest typist in the world, or he typed and deleted a few versions of this.

Text to Chase: Want to hang out sometime?

Text from Chase: With me? What happened with not normally dating guys like me?

Text to Chase: I understand if I'm too late. I'll fuck off now.

Text from Chase: No!

Text to Chase: But you can't rub it in to Leo and Jeff. Got it?

Text from Chase: I can't tell Leo at all?

Text to Chase: Forget it.

Text from Chase: I'm kidding. Tell me where and when. I'll be there.

I look around my living room, wondering how different it's going to look in another year. Will it be full of baby toys if I can afford them? I stare at my phone. I bet Chase would be the kind of dad who'd buy his kid every toy and enjoy going to the toy store.

Text to Chase: Do you know a place that serves peanut butter and jelly?

Chapter 10

CHASE

She looks beautiful – glowing even - and she sure looks like she feels better. Maybe she's just happy to hang out with me. Liam must have put in a good word for me, so I owe him big if that's the case. Lorelei, too.

I'm so excited that I almost forgot to put deodorant on, as meticulous as I was with other aspects of my grooming. I spent nearly an hour in front of my mirror, fixing my hair into a style that looked like I hadn't spent any time on it at all and trying on eight shirts before finally settling on one in royal blue that brings out the color of my eyes.

Did she spend as much time on herself as I did?

I glance at her dress, a pink V-neck that dips low. Her boobs look magnificent in it. Full. Fuck I'd motorboat the hell out of them if I ever get so lucky as to put my face anywhere near them again.

Her cheeks are a rosy pink, and part of me wonders if she's flushed. "Are you hot? I can ask the waiter to adjust the temperature?"

She shakes her head and looks at something over my shoulder. For a woman who asked me out, she seems distant – like she doesn't want to look at me.

"So, Lorelei and Liam are getting pretty serious, huh?" I ask in a desperate attempt to talk to her. "Think they'll have babies soon?"

Her eyes flick to mine with a panicked look. What'd I say to cause that distress? I hold my hands up. "Just kidding. Fuck, could you imagine that shit?" I fake shiver. "A little Liam running around, judging people for God knows what? He'd have a little tape measure and obnoxiously click it to make sure people comply with the law. Who needs that?"

She blinks and smiles. I don't know her that well, but I know it's not a real smile. It doesn't reach her eyes or make her squint like I've seen her do when her students make her laugh.

I nervously tap the table and look around our booth like the sugar packets are going to inspire a conversation. I inhale through my nose and blow it out as I wrack my brain on something to talk about. I need to take charge of the situation.

I clear my throat and drop my voice to something I hope calms her. "Thanks for texting me and giving me a chance to get to know you, Kailee. I'm really happy to be out with you."

Her shoulders slump a bit like she's relaxing, and my heart slows its rampant pounding. Maybe I have a chance if I can just assure her that I'm here to get to know her. I should apologize for being a dick earlier at work. Would she even listen?

"Chase," she says. I lean toward her, showing her I am ready to listen to any anecdote or joke she throws at me. If I show women a smidge of attention, they're all over my dick. At least, that's how it's worked on dates in the past.

"Yes?" I ask after a few seconds pass without her saying any-thing. "Is there something you want to say?"

She blinks and quickly looks back at her menu. Too quickly. "What are you getting? Everything looks delicious. Mmm. I'm starving."

Odd. I could have sworn she was going to tell me something profound.

"Is there something you want to ask me?"

I know we went through basics like favorite colors the night we met, and she knows who my friends are and what I do for a living. But I expected her to have the normal first date questions about my favorite TV shows or my first car. Maybe my family or which high school sports I played.

She shakes her head and frowns. "Nope. Nothing. Nada. Zip. Zero. Zilch."

I look back at my own menu. "You mentioned something about peanut butter and jelly? Is that your favorite food?"

"No, I..." her voice trails off. She leans forward and looks at me pointedly, her eyes unblinking and round. "I had a *craving*. You know, *cravings*?"

"Ha! I get that. I occasionally have a craving for chicken nuggets. For some reason, I also *have* to eat Chinese food on a stakeout. It's a thing with Liam and me. We have this hookup, Mr. Lau, and he delivers Chinese to us whenever we're working. Liam and I saved his son from getting further into a gang with some heavy drug usage. He's promised us Chinese food for life when we're working. We tried to turn him down, but no joke, he kept showing up at the station randomly with full bags of food until we told him we'd really call him when we're hungry." I shrug as she watches me with a neutral expression. "We called him a couple of times, and now I associate Chinese food with late-night stakeouts."

She tilts her head to the side, and I almost gasp with happiness because it's the first time since the night we met that she seems generally interested in what I'm saying.

My heart pounds hard again as I search my mind for something else to say. Something to entertain her. If necessary, I'd tap dance on the table to keep her attention.

The waitress comes to the table to take our order. The place we're eating is an upscale sandwich shop. I thought Kailee was kidding about the peanut butter and jelly, but she quickly orders it from the kid's menu with a glass of water, a glass of Sprite, and saltines on the side.

Gosh, you really get to know someone when you're on a dinner date. But hey, at least she's not hiding who she is and what she likes.

I quickly order a pot roast sandwich with extra horseradish and a bowl of chicken, rice, and vegetable soup. After the waitress leaves, I lean my elbows on the table and focus on Kailee. I want to get to know her. That's why we're here. I'm not getting any action tonight. I'm banning myself from it. This night is about listening to Kailee and finding out what she wants in a boyfriend. If I can piece that together, maybe I'll have a shot at applying for the job.

She fiddles with her silverware as soon as we're alone, and I force the grin onto my face. I probably look like a serial killer. Clearing my throat, I finally lean across the table and grab her hand, stilling her fork before she can tap it on the table again. "Why are you nervous tonight?" I ask.

She reddens and looks down before dropping the cutlery to the table with a clatter. "This isn't a normal first date, Chase."

I squint and stroke my thumb over the top of her hand. Her whole body shivers at my light touch, and the vibration moves through my forearm, waking up my dick in the process. "What do you mean? You went out with Leo. I can't assume that was your first date."

She blows out a sigh so hard that the hair framing her face moves. "I've been on a million first dates, Chase..." She trails off, and she looks at the wall behind me. She opens her mouth, then closes it again. "I just feel like there's a lot at stake."

"Because our friends are together, and we're stuck in each other's orbit if they get married?"

"Yes."

"Because we already had incredibly hot sex and it feels like we're doing this out of order?"

"Also true."

"Did I miss one?"

The waitress comes with our food just as Kailee starts to reply. She looks disappointed as the waitress places her food in front of her and then hands me a steaming tray of hot meat. I inhale dramatically as the waitress sets the soup in front of me and walks away. "Want a bite of mine?"

Kailee doesn't look at my plate, but she shakes her head so dramatically that I'd hear her jowls slap if she was an old lady.

"What were we talking about?" I ask, stirring my soup.

"Nothing exciting," she says like she's trying to change the subject. "Do you really think it's going that well with Lorelei and Liam?"

I take a bite of my sandwich and allow my shoulders to droop in a swoon before answering. "I think they'll be married by next Tuesday. You?"

"Definitely not getting married next Tuesday."

I laugh. Hey, at least she made a joke. Maybe she'll open up now. "Do you think Liam is the one for your girl?"

She shrugs and takes a tentative bite of her food. She swallows, and it looks forced. Does her throat hurt?

I tilt my head in concern, and she notices the frown. She quickly takes another bite and smiles at me as she chews. "Umm. Good," she mutters around the mouthful.

I focus on my own food as she takes a few more quiet bites. "I'd go next Monday," she eventually says, answering my Liam and Lorelei question.

"Yeah. They're in love, and it's pretty obvious he's been in love with her since they met."

She lifts one of her eyebrows. "Do you think that's possible? Love at first meeting, I mean?"

I'm the one who looks down at my food away from her eyes this time. "Maybe. I've never felt it before, but I know Liam got hit in the face with a board by your best friend." I pause, my spoon frozen halfway to my mouth. "Have you felt it?"

"The lightning strike?" she asks.

"The board to the face."

She smiles. "I'm not sure," she whispers.

"Yeah, actually, I'd like to change my answer. When I said it's never happened before, I can't say that's true."

"Why?" she asks.

"I met you, and it was like magic, Kailee."

She sets her sandwich down. "You can't be in love with me. We don't know each other."

I hold up my hands. "I didn't say love. I just..." I search for the words as she leans over her plate, so far that her tits may end up with peanut butter on them. Damn. Now my dick's paying attention again. "I just think that we would have had a shot, you know? A real chance," I say. "You're the first person in a long time that I met and want to get to know better. That doesn't happen often for me."

A loose strand of hair falls around her neck, and my fingers itch to push it behind her ear. "Kailee, If you wouldn't have run that morning, and if we'd have had breakfast, we would have showered together and gone to the farmer's market or something. I think we would've had a chance, and that is what I want this to be." I flick my hand, gesturing to the table. "If you want to run out of the restaurant screaming and run right to Leo or Jeff, or whatever dickbag wants you, I understand. But you're the first person I've met in a long time who I want to try with. I want to know what you were thinking when you ran. Did you expect me to kick you out?"

"Yes," she says, her eyes watering a bit. "When I have a one-night stand, the men either ask me to leave right after...you know, or they push me out the door with a canned protein shake and a smile the next morning. You would have been the first for a farmer's market visit."

I lean forward until we're eye to eye and I'm concerned about my own shirt getting soup on it. "Then it was a first for us both because I usually don't give one shit about the women in my bed, but I damn well give a shit about you, and I have no idea why."

Kailee leans back and looks at her food again. I start eating my own, and I wait for her to say something – wait for her to take the lead here.

But she never does. We finish our food in silence.

When the check comes, I pounce on it before she can grab it, leave enough cash for the food and a tip, and then help her into her light jacket. She shivers again as I slide my hands down her shoulders, and I walk her out in the misting rain, sliding my hand into hers before we reach the car.

We ride in silence to her place, neither of us knowing what to say. But it feels right. It's almost like being on a long car ride with an old friend – a friend you know so well that you can happily exist in silence next to them. It's how I feel with Liam on stakeouts. It's how I feel when my parents come to town. After telling them all the goings on of my life, we can be next to each other without bombarding the group with questions.

My hand is on the gear shift, and she caresses the top of my hand, tracing my veins with her index finger. It relaxes me so much that my eyes flutter, and I almost miss the green light. As we merge onto the interstate, she leans over, sighs, and rests her head on my shoulder. I wrap my free arm around her and play with the ends of her hair, marveling that they're like silk in my fingers.

I will stop at the bridge ahead and jump out right here and now if Leo Paulson got to touch this hair. This is her hair, but I want this to be only mine for touching. Like a little secret we both have.

I kiss the top of her head and slowly merge back onto a two-lane road at the next exit. My entire body tingles as she puts her hand on my leg as I pull into her apartment complex's visitor parking.

She lifts her head, blinking like she's not sure how we got home so fast. "Thanks for picking me up."

"A gentleman always picks a woman up," I say, unbuckling my seatbelt. "And a gentleman always makes sure a lady gets inside safely. Let me walk you in."

She nods and gets out of the car before I can get around the car to open the door. I get to her in time to offer her my hand like my mother taught me to do when helping a woman from a seated position. "Thanks for a nice night," I say, walking her to the door.

She turns to face me, stopping suddenly. "Was it nice? I feel like it was short. You picked me up, we did small talk, we ate sandwiches, and now we're back. Is that enough to even be considered a first date?"

Here it is. Is she going to ask me in?

I nod. "It's enough for now. We'll do more next time. I meant what I said, Kailee. I would have spent more time with you from the get-go. I want to get to know you. I'll make the second date something really cool."

She places her hands on my chest, and my skin burns with her touch, even through my shirt. I bite my bottom lip to keep from picking her up, throwing her over my shoulder, and taking her to bed.

"I shouldn't have run away. I assumed you were like all the rest."

"I am like all the rest," I say. She jolts and shakes her head like she's waking up from a dream. I lean forward, brushing my lips over her jaw and dropping my chin to match my voice. "But not with you."

She pushes her forehead to my chest, and I let her stand there. I like the feel of her in my arms. She's like my childhood stuffed panda I carried until I was six. Safe. For some reason, she's comforting. If anyone attacked us right this second, I'd protect her at all costs, but right now, she's keeping me safe from feeling like I'm not loveable. I always thought I was broken in that way because I never had what Liam and Lorelei seem to have.

I want it so very badly, and I want it with this woman.

"Will you come in?" she asks softly. "I can't run away since it's my place."

I chuckle and put my finger under her chin, tilting her face up to mine. "Not tonight. Let's do this right this time. Let's leave our first date and not get physical tonight."

She whimpers, and her eyes flutter as I drag my finger up her cheek. With my other hand, I gently fist her hair, leaning her back even further. Her eyes shut, and her lips open slightly with the expectation of my lips on hers.

I don't disappoint. I don't crush her lips like we kissed when we had sex, but she knows I'm not fucking around. I'm firm, telling her that her lips are mine from now on if she'll have me. Her arms wind around my neck as I bend my frame to meet her mouth without her standing on her tiptoes. My free hand not in her hair cups her cheek, and I taste her – the sweet taste of the jelly she licked off her sandwich bread mixed with the taste I recognize as distinctly hers.

I remember her taste. The feel of her hand in my hair. Her soft whimpers as my tongue explores her mouth. I remember the warmth of her hair against my fingers, and my cock begs me to reconsider her offer.

She wobbles a bit, and I move my hand from her hair to her waist, ready to catch her as I internally congratulate myself on making this woman, the one I choose, weak in the knees from a kiss.

I pull my lips away, and she keeps her eyes closed, searching for my mouth again with her own. I miss the connection, but I won't be swayed tonight. Someday in the future, I'll make love to her five different ways.

We'll sleep alone tonight.

I press my forehead to hers and reach into the top of her purse until I find her door keys. She lets me pull them out and open her door for her. Only when she's safely inside, still pink in the cheeks from kissing me, do I drop one last kiss on her forehead. "Goodnight, Kailee. I'll see you at work."

Chapter 11

CHASE

This walking around shit is getting old. So far today, I've caught two vapers in the boys' bathroom and have eaten way too many bags of chips from the vending machine. I'd kill for an interesting incident like the one last week where I busted up a sex ring in the staff bathroom. Not amongst the staff. Apparently, a group of juniors figured out the code for the staff bathroom and arranged with their partners to get out of class at the exact same time. Caught them red-handed, and I'm not sure which of us was more embarrassed at that.

Just another day working in a high school.

I haven't seen Kailee as much as I'd like for the last few days. I walk by her classroom at least twice a day and watch her through the window. I wave at her, and she waves back, earning all kinds of sounds from the students in her room. She waves them off and returns to teaching as I stare through the window like a lost puppy for a few seconds

When it comes to her, I am a lost puppy.

Lost.

Infatuated.

Totally fucked.

I've tried catching her in the teacher's lounge, but I can only assume she's avoiding it for some reason. I'm not sure why she's avoiding the other teachers while they eat, but I'm hopeful she's not avoiding me.

After the last bell rings for the day, I head to the vending machine again, hopeful the guy who comes to fill it has been by and restocked the Snickers bars. The place is empty, with most teachers staying in their classrooms and packing up at the end of the day. But I have nothing to go home to. Some days, it's nice to roam the quiet hallways here. Sometimes I go into Kailee's classroom after she's left work and just sit in her chair, sniffing the air for traces of her perfume.

I close the door to the teacher's lounge and shuffle down the hallway, daydreaming about what it would be like to have Kailee waiting for me at home – or even being home when she came in from work. My daydream takes me to the recipes I'd cook for her and our conversations over a candlelight dinner I'd make.

I can't get her out of my head. Never have been able to. I'm so consumed that I almost miss the soft sound of someone crying as I pass the teacher workroom.

I stop in my tracks, and I turn my ear toward the door, hoping I'm just hearing things. Stepping closer, the distinct sound of sniffling can be heard from the other side of the pine door. A whimper follows it.

I knock lightly before gently pushing the door open. "Resource officer. Just clearing the room," I say while the door is slightly cracked. I don't want to interrupt or embarrass a staff member.

"Chase?" a weak voice asks.

I know that voice. I don't give a fuck about the door as I fling it open so hard it hits the wall only to find a red-faced and tear-stained Kailee standing in the room holding construction paper.

"Kailee?" I ask, my voice husky with worry. "Is that you crying?"

I cringe as soon as I ask the question. She's obviously been crying. She's alone, and her face is so swollen that I worry she's having an allergic reaction to something. I even look around the room like I'm going to find random shellfish or another common allergen.

"Yeah," she says, walking to me. Her arms are out, and I take her into my own arms, wrapping them around her so tight that I have to pull back a little lest I hurt her. I bury my face in her hair as she sobs against me, her shoulders shaking.

I'm powerless as I rub her back and kiss the crown of her head every few seconds. A dizzying amount of emotions and questions hit me all at once.

Anger.

Did someone hurt her?

Fear.

Is she mad at me?

Anger again.

Who do I kill first? Leo or Jeff?

Annoyance.

Did a student make her cry? If so, I'll give them so many de-tentions their family will think they got a side job after school.

Empathy.

Whatever is upsetting her, I'll gladly take the burden from her if I can.

Eventually, her grip around my waist loosens, and she nods. I even let her wipe her eyes on my shirt, not caring one little bit about the wetness now on my chest. Once she steps back from me, I bend to her level and cup her cheeks, forcing her to look at me. "Who hurt you?"

She sputters a laugh from her mouth. "I'm not hurt. I –

Her voice cuts off and her face crinkles again. "I just have a lot on my plate right now. I don't know how to t-tell y-you," she stammers. She holds on to my wrist, and her fingers tremble against my skin.

"Tell me what, Kailee?"

She's silent for a moment, and I straighten with a frown. I pinch my nose and shake my head. "I'm too late, aren't I?"

"W-what?" she asks.

"Are you going out with Leo again? Look, if you like him, just tell me. I don't like it, but I'll back off."

Back off my ass. I'll go home and hit my punching bag I keep in my garage until my knuckles bleed.

She waves her hands in front of her face. "It's not Leo."

I blow out a breath of relief. "Then what is it?"

She stares at me for what seems like an infinite amount of time but is probably only a few seconds. I swallow as I feel the room contract. She's going to tell me she doesn't have time for me. She wants to see someone else. If we don't work out, we'll never be able to hang out with Liam and Lorelei together, so it's best if we don't even try.

I straighten my shoulders and flex my jaw. Maybe I'm too scary because she backs away and swallows. "I'm just having a rough day. I guess I'm stressed with this job and all the responsibilities real teachers have." She nods to the construction paper and wipes her nose. "I came down to make makeshift recipe cards because the kids are all out of index cards, and I don't feel like I can ask their families to buy more at this point in the quarter."

My eyes flick around the room and then back to her. Stepping forward, I wipe a piece of hair out of her face. "Need help?"

She breathes in, and her breath does that choppy shaking thing mine did when I was a child and had a really hard cry. She wipes her face again and looks at the paper trimmer. It's the kind with a machete-like knife that my friends and I used to play paper doll guillotine with in third grade when the teacher wasn't looking.

She slides her hand down my chest and simultaneously sends chills down my body. "Can you stay and keep me company?" she asks. "Lately, I've been...tired of being alone."

"Of course," I mumble.

I follow her to the station and run my hand up her back as she picks up a small stack of construction paper and situates it in the cutter. She's still sniffling a little, so I move my hand to her neck. "Want a massage?" I ask, already running my hand over her warm skin.

She slouches and rolls her neck against my palm. "Yes," she squeaks.

"Come here." I pull her closer to me until my face is in her hair and my hands work her shoulders. "You shouldn't be so stressed."

She sniffs again and wipes her nose. "I just don't know what to do, Chase."

"I know your job is stressful, but sometimes you just have to let people help."

She rolls her neck again. I can hardly think straight while I'm touching her. Her skin is too warm. Too soft. My cock thumps at my zipper, telling me to shit or get off the pot when it comes to this woman. I run my eyes down the length of her body at the pencil skirt she's wearing. I could just lift it up a little right here, right now in the school workroom. Just move her panties to the side and slide into home...

Home.

Lust washes over me, and her body tenses in what I hope is a sign of the feeling being mutual.

"Kailee," I whisper as I move her hair aside and drop a soft kiss on her collarbone. "I want you so fucking bad. I can't help it."

She stiffens a bit. "Here?"

"Here."

She turns her face to the door, probably waiting for someone to burst through. "We'd get caught."

"No. Students are gone. Activities aren't in this part of the building on Wednesdays. All the teachers are leaving. It's just us. You don't want me?"

"I do," she whines, sliding her hand up my cheek. She hasn't turned to look at me, but she shakes against my chest, and I pull her tighter. "I want you, Chase. I wanted you the other night."

"Me too, baby, but I wanted to be respectful of a first date with you. You deserved that. But now that I have you trapped in the teacher workroom, I very much want to slide my hands up this little skirt and pull your wet panties aside. You know how good I can make it."

She bites her lip, adorably whimpers my name, and I double down. I remove my service weapon, check the safety, and then set it on the table before doing the same with my taser and removing my entire police belt, moving slowly to let her hear the sound of the metal as I get myself ready. I run my zipper down its track, teasing her with the sound until she finally turns to face me.

Her mouth is on mine, and her hands wind through my hair. I kiss her back, breathlessly and with a hunger I've only felt with her the first time we met. This is no polite goodnight kiss like the other night.

I reach down and slide her skirt up to her waist at the same time she digs through my pants and pulls my already hard and wet dick from the confines of my boxer briefs. We're ravenous for each other, and if we were at home, I'd tear her shirt off and watch the buttons roll across my living room.

But it's not the time nor the place for that.

I pick her up and walk us to the nearest wall. No countertop this time. No bending her over. I want her face-to-face, with her legs wrapped around me while I push into her. I want to watch her eyes when I make her come. I want to watch my cum drip down her legs when I'm done.

She adjusts her skirt until it's around her waist, checks the door once more, and then lets the moment overtake her. Part of the allure of all of this is the possibility of getting caught, even though I know it's unlikely.

I push my pants down far enough to work and lift her so she has to wrap her legs around me. Moving her panties to the side, I take a second to appreciate just how wet they are. "Mmm. Someone likes this idea more than they've let on," I whisper in her ear.

Her reply is her fingernails digging into the back of my neck as I push inside her tight pussy. I relish the pain, though. I know there will be marks tomorrow, but they'll be *her* marks. I'll take bite marks, nail lines up my back, and whatever else she wants to torture me with. I'm totally hers if she'll have me.

"Kailee," I moan against her neck. "Fuck, baby, we could have been doing this all along if someone wasn't so damn stubborn."

She ignores my comment and bucks against me like a wild woman. I speed up my thrusts to match her want. She's unhinged, pulling at my hair as I push into her.

Hard.

If I keep this up, I'll come way too fast.

Sliding out of her warmth, I drop to my knees in front of her as she groans in frustration. She grips my hair and looks down at me. "Come back," she begs.

"In a minute, sweetheart."

I pull her leg until it's over my shoulder and place my hand on her abdomen, holding her in place. She stiffens, and I look up, wondering if I did something wrong. She gives me a weak smile and then moves my hand up her stomach a little until it's right under her ribs. Does she want me to play with her breasts?

Yeah, well I want to play with her pussy.

I push my face into her slit, pulling her panties completely off with a loud tearing sound. I pause for a second, unsure what to do with them now that they're in my hand, and I settle on pushing them into my pants pocket.

I lick, lap, and love on her clit as she holds onto me, lest she slide to the floor. The salty taste of her skin combined with the sweet taste of her want rolls over my tongue, and I swoon and hum against her in utter rapture. I could eat her forever. It's like Halloween candy and Thanksgiving turkey rolled into one meal. A perfect combination of sweet and savory rolling over my tongue.

Her legs stiffen until I worry she'll buckle, so I grip her hips, holding her against the wall as she shatters, whining my name and biting her lip so she won't yell. Her head thrashes from side to side against the cool wall, and I lick her until every single tremble is done, leaving her a panting mess above me.

Sliding up her body, I kiss her belly and then kiss her breasts through her shirt. When I reach her mouth again, I run my tongue over her lips and smile against her skin. "You taste good."

She's like a limp rag now, but she still puts her arms around my neck as I position her the way I want her – legs around me and looking into my eyes.

I slide into her, and our eyes lock. It's all I can do not to close my eyes as the feel of her wet heat around me has my balls already high and tight. "Kailee, I've wanted this for months. I would have done this to you all that time if you would have let me. Are you going to let me now?" I finish the question with a deep thrust, taunting her. "Huh, baby?"

"Yes," she moans.

She bends to my shoulder and bites me. Hard. Punishment for not coming after her the first time she ran away? Not getting her number from Liam and tracking her down at all costs?

Whatever it is, I don't think about it too long as my orgasm coils like a cornered snake. My body contracts and then relaxes as I moan and release inside of her, growling her name against her jaw.

Once I'm spent, I pull away and drop to the floor again to plant a kiss on her hip and watch my cum drip down her legs, even as she hustles her skirt down her hips in case someone comes in.

"You're worried now?" I chuckle, playfully biting down her leg.

"I was worried before, but now that we're both done, there's no use tempting fate."

"Come on," I say, kissing her knee once and then getting up from the floor. I pull my pants up and fit my softening dick back into my underwear. "I'm a drug task force agent and still alive. When have I ever lost when I tempted fate?"

Chapter 12

KAILEE

It's a strange feeling when your stomach tells you that there's a good chance you'll die of starvation if you don't eat. Then, when you eat, it tells you there's an even better chance that you'll die from throwing it all up.

After the incident in the teacher's workroom, I haven't seen Chase for a couple of days. I'm not quite sure what to do with the knowledge that we're still sexually attracted to each other, so I've been the one intentionally keeping out of his path. He's oblivious to my plight of deciding whether to continue incubating our combined cells, and the further I step into our burgeoning relationship, the harder it is to tell him I'm pregnant. It's like meeting someone, interacting with them daily, and then asking them to remind you what their name is three months later. At some point, it's just awkward.

I almost told him in the workroom. But then he stiffened, and a dark look came over his face. I got scared. I couldn't have the conversation at work. Then, we did what we did, thus complicating things further while also showing me that pregnancy sex is insane.

Text from Chase: You hungry?

As soon as I read his message, my stomach roils at the very idea of food. All except for one kind.

Text to Chase: Just for the usual.

Text from Chase: Me?

Text to Chase: Funny. Nah. My usual sandwich. But I'm just staying in tonight. I haven't felt great today.

I drop my phone onto my coffee table and pull the blanket over me. I mean to rest my eyes for a minute, but the next thing I know, there's a light knocking sound at my door. I pick up the phone and see several missed messages from Chase over the last hour.

I'm so fucking tired of being so fucking tired.

I swipe my hand over my face to catch any stray drool and stumble to the door, kicking throw pillows that have ended up on my floor aside. When I make it to the door, I fling it open, my lips parted and ready to berate Lorelei for interrupting my nap.

It's not Lorelei.

"Your peanut butter and jelly sandwich, my lady," Chase says, his bicep oddly close to my face as he leans against my doorframe.

I slouch against my wall, probably from weakness since I haven't wanted much today except for queen olives, which sounded oddly enticing, and ten pieces of pepperoni. Chase shakes a takeout bag from the place we went on our date, and I tear it from his hands.

"You sure love peanut butter and jelly more than anyone I've ever known." He shuts the door and follows me into the apartment. "Have you always liked it that much?"

"This is a new thing."

I plop on the couch and quickly unwrap the sandwich. As soon as I bite down, I know that there's a multiverse somewhere out there where I've married Chase Barnett.

"I swear to God, this is *suck your dick* good," I mumble, chewing around the doughy white bread. It's soft and practically melts in my mouth. I can feel the gluten as it rolls over my tongue with the salty goodness of the peanut butter and the sweetness of the organic strawberry jelly the shop gets from a local woman.

Chase gently sits on my couch and watches me attack my food like he's at the zoo for feeding time – with mild amusement. "Suck my dick good, huh?" He adjusts his cock and smiles at me, jerking his chin. "Leave the peanut butter in your mouth when you do it."

"Pig."

"I get that a lot as a cop." He crosses his feet on my coffee table. "You'll have to do better than that when you insult me. It loses its bite after the hundredth time we hear it."

"Noted," I say around another mouthful of salty and sugary goodness.

He's quiet for a few moments as he strokes my back. I take two more bites and turn to face him. "Thanks. It really is becoming my favorite. I don't know what it is about peanut butter, but I can't get enough."

"I can't get enough of you," he whispers.

How can he look at me like that? Most of the time, I feel like an extra stumbling out of the set for *The Walking Dead*. He studies me with so much affection. I know he'd bend me over the sofa arm right here. His eyes are dark and hooded. His nostrils flare. Why? I look like...well, I look like a woman who's finishing a rough first trimester, gets little sleep, and has only eaten olives and pepperoni today.

Damn, he actually looks good. Is this what my book meant when it said women are horny while pregnant? Because I have the overwhelming urge to curl up in his lap, kiss his face and neck, and work my way down. Even the idea of blowing him doesn't sound so bad. The olives, peanut butter, and pepperoni all have one thing in common.

Salt.

I know the salty goodness that is Chase Barnett's dick. I tasted it in the wee hours of the morning the first time we met.

Before I ran away.

I chew my sandwich with renewed interest in what I jokingly suggested. After another glorious bite, I set my sandwich down and wipe my hands on my thighs. "Chase, could you do me a favor?"

"Anything."

"Can you go to the pantry and get my peanut butter?"

He's off the sofa and at the pantry door in a few short steps. When he returns, he sets it on the coffee table. "Did the sandwich I got you not have enough peanut butter on it? Need a knife?"

"Let's use a spoon for this."

No use risking an injury.

He shrugs and goes to the kitchen to get me the spoon, balancing it on top of the bulk-sized container when he comes back. "Here you go, Kailee."

God, he says it with so much innocence, and I know he's anything but. This man has done vile things to me in his house and at work, but he has no idea what I want. I want him in my mouth with salty, peanutty goodness around his dick so bad that I wipe a spot of drool from the corner of my mouth.

"Sit back and undo your pants."

He cocks his head to the side before flicking his eyes to the peanut butter. "Um, are you joking?"

"Do I seem like a woman who jokes about my love of peanut butter? And I owe you a little something for the other day. If a man brings a lady a sandwich, he's going to get something fun in return." I run my eyes up his body. "You may want to take your shirt off, too."

Chase looks around the couch. "Should we put down some plastic wrap or something?"

He's not wrong. This could get mushy and wet. I look for something nearby, frantically wishing I'm the kind of woman who buys plastic wrap. I don't have anything but aluminum foil in the kitchen, but I do have plastic placemats Lorelei bought me for a housewarming gift when I moved into this rat trap.

I grab one I use for soup and cups of tea off my coffee table, all while congratulating myself that I don't own proper coasters. Quickly, I tuck it under Chase's thighs, and he lifts himself off the couch so I can situate it under him.

If he thinks I'm weird, he doesn't let on. In fact, I've never seen a man remove his shirt so quickly. He unbuckles his belt as he watches me get on my knees in front of him. "I can't decide if you're an angel or the devil himself," he says.

I grab the spoon and peanut butter jar off the coffee table before he stops me, his hand coming to my wrist. "We don't need the spoon."

I frown and eye the jar in confusion. "Don't you want me to spread it on your dick?" I ask.

"If we're going to be dirty rebels, we're going to do it right. I'm going to stick my dick in the peanut butter jar like it's the finger I always got scolded for as a kid."

"You got in trouble for that?"

"All the time. Give me that jar. I'll bring you a new one to work tomorrow."

I hand it over, watching with rapt fascination as Chase screws the top off the jar and wastes no time dipping his already erect cock into the substance. There's a slight squishing noise, but Chase covers the sound with his own moan as he throws his head back. "Fuck, you bought the crunchy kind. Are you trying to drive me insane?"

"Not what I was thinking when I used the coupon for it."

He bites his lip. "Fuck, the little nuts scrape me just right. This is nice. I should use this at home."

"Well, let's hope Liam doesn't ever want to make a sandwich with your edible pocket pussy while he's over there."

He lifts his head, focuses his eyes, and chuckles as he strokes my hair, pushing a strand back. I remove the elastic I always have on my wrist and quickly put my hair up before I pull the jar away from him.

There's a sucking sound, and Chase's cock is in front of me, covered from tip to root in crunchy peanut butter.

I grip the base of his length and flex my fingers around him, getting used to the peanut butter as it oozes between my fingers. As soon as I'm used to the sensation and confirm I have a grip on him, I fist him, jerking him up and down, slow at first and also putting my wrist into the action with a twisting motion.

The peanut butter slides through my fingers, but the placemat was a good idea because the brown goo runs down Chase's balls and drips somewhere I can't see. I lift his dick, and he spreads his thighs in anticipation of what he's going to get.

I don't disappoint him. I take one salty ball into my mouth and suck on it, flicking my tongue and humming with pleasure at the taste of him. It's like having a peanut butter and Chase sandwich. Salt on top of salt.

He fists my hair at the base of my ponytail and takes deep breaths as I work the other ball over, lapping and sucking as my hand continues jerking him. "Taste good, Kailee? Is that what you were hungry for?"

I snort laugh a little as I release his sack from my mouth. "Yep. I woke up wanting your balls slathered in peanut butter."

He doesn't respond. His head tilts back, and I can only see his throat as he swallows and takes deep gulps of air. I place my free hand on the happy trail on his abdomen and flex my fingers over his abdominal muscles as they tense and release in the same rhythm as my hand.

When I've licked the peanut butter off his balls, I move to his dick. I take the head in my mouth and suck, making yummy noises because...fuck, it tastes good. I'm so hungry, and his dick is covered in the one thing I can stomach well and the one thing

I want. I'm starving. Starving for him and starving for the one food I can stomach.

Peanut butter smears my face all the way up to my nose. My cheeks itch with it, but I don't dare swipe it away. For one, I'd just make it worse. I have peanut butter all over my hands. Second, I want him to see me dirty and completely covered for him. I want him to see the lengths I'll go to for a messy blow job.

It's a lot, though. I can't suck and swallow all of it, and brown drool runs down his cock every time I bob. I take him further, trying to catch my spit with long laps, but it's a fruitless effort as some gets away and drips onto the placemat.

Chase's ass clenches, and his back bows off the couch. He moans, and the sound wakes my clit along with my nipples, my blood roaring to life in my veins. The smell of his skin, all man, mixes with the food, and I hungrily suck him like a woman eating food for the first time in weeks.

His abdominal muscles tighten against my forehead, and I drop low, almost to the point of gagging. Thankfully, I hold it in, and I hollow out my cheeks for him as his butt cheeks clench. He fists my ponytail harder, and I speed up my head bobs.

"Kailee, I'm going to come. I'm going to come so fucking hard. Your mouth...Fuck, baby."

He whimpers, and my chest blooms with pride. This tall, gorgeous Viking cop that is a hero to this town for many things is covered with my own food and losing his shit in my mouth.

I pull away from him just as his balls tighten and twitch. This isn't my first rodeo, and I know what that means. I'm usually a swallow kind of gal, but I don't know if my stomach can handle anything but the food I'm in love with this week, and I do not want to throw up on Chase Barnett.

He moans through his orgasm, and his eyes are hooded as he watches his cum coat my face, hitting my cheeks and even my eyelashes. I squint but don't dare swipe at my eyes. When he's spent, he runs his dick down my sticky cheek, practically purring at me.

We both catch our breath until my knees officially protest, and I think to check the placemat. As soon as Chase lifts off the couch, he gets up and waddles to my kitchen, bringing back a roll of paper towels. "Don't move. I'll get the big stuff off your face," he whispers as he wipes both his dick and balls with one wad of towels and my eyes and down my cheeks with the other. Once we're semi-clean, we both silently wash up in the kitchen sink.

Chase runs a wet paper towel over his balls, and a chuckle comes from my throat. I clap my hands over my mouth because I can't contain the laughter of a gorgeous man wiping his balls in my kitchen.

"Oh, you think that's funny, huh?" he taunts, nuzzling my cheek. "You should see your face. You have some in your hair."

I run my wet paper towel through the strands he points to, and I eventually give up, throwing my paper towel into the nearby trashcan with a huff. "What's the use? I'll need a full shower."

"I think I may have some in my butthole," Chase murmurs, eliciting more laughter from me until we're both doubled over and frantically wiping drying peanut butter from our skin.

"Want a shower?" I ask when I can finally talk and breathe again. A dark look crosses his face, and I step away from him wide-eyed. I shake my head. "Don't even think about whatever you're thinking about, Chase." I point my finger in his face, giggling.

He steps toward me, backing me into the wall. "What do you think I'm thinking about?"

"Getting me back somehow." I try to playfully push him away but he boxes me in, kissing my cheeks, nose, and anywhere he can reach as I struggle against his size.

Before I can fight him off, he lifts me over his shoulder. I kick my feet and lightly pummel his back, jokingly demanding I be set down immediately. I'm like a sack of flour, and I momentarily worry about his shoulder lodged into my stomach. It's uncomfortable, and I worry about the baby for the briefest of seconds before he stomps to my room, kicking the door open and quickly laying me on the bed as he fumbles through the room in the dark. As soon as I'm settled on the top of the blanket, he runs his hand down the front of me from my chin to the waistband of my pants. "We'll shower in a few minutes," he says. "I'm kind of hungry myself."

I reach for his hand, but he's suddenly not there. He's at the door and silhouetted in the moonlight coming through my blinds. "What are you doing?"

"I'll be right back. I need something."

"What?" We sure don't need a condom, but I'm not sure how I can say that now. It's never the right time with him.

He laughs and disappears toward my kitchen. I hear the unmistakable sound of my fridge opening and Chase rummaging around my condiment shelves. When he comes back, he holds up a jar of something as he walks back to me.

"For someone who likes peanut butter and jelly so much, you don't have any jelly."

"Then what's in your hand?" I ask, squinting.

"You're lucky I like marmalade, Kailee."

I put my finger up. "That can't come anywhere near my lady bits downstairs, Chase. I mean it. I do not need a doctor's appointment or a bladder infection this week."

He smiles and walks like a panther toward me. "Your call, but it'll still look nice on your tits."

Chapter 13

KAILEE

"You two came together?" Lorelei asks, taking a plastic container of dip out of my hands and patting Chase on the shoulder as he walks into her house.

I wait until he's a few feet away. "Boy, did we ever."

She stifles her laugh with a fist over her mouth, and I watch as Liam clinks beer bottles with Chase. I feel long forgotten as Chase blends into his coworkers like he can't wait to see and talk to them. I don't blame him. I don't think he's meant to work in a school with mostly nice teenagers. He belongs out in the world, making sure it's safe from hard drugs and the people who take advantage of those with addiction. It's who he is, and I know he's happy that Liam's back at work after the close call with death. Chase whistled the whole time he got ready at my apartment this evening.

Lorelei thought she'd have a party to welcome Liam back to the drug task force world. After several weeks of physical therapy and counseling, he's ready to be back in a limited capacity until the investigation of weapons usage is complete for both of them. Chase will be leaving the high school soon, too.

Deep sadness sinks into my stomach that I won't see him every day after next week. Our regular resource officer will be back in action, his shingles recovering nicely, and it'll be time for Chase to report to work at the sheriff's office. Sure, he's been back for his own rounds of counseling and reporting on the incident, but that's only been an hour at a time. For someone I was trying to avoid for a good chunk of the last month, I'll sure miss him now that he leaves me random treats and always has a smile for me.

"Come into the kitchen with me and help," Lorelei says, waving her hand in front of my face and waking me from wherever my brain went with thinking about Chase. "We can talk and not have all these police officers breathing down our necks."

I follow her as she leads me through her very pink house, and I wonder if that will change when Liam moves in soon. Will he replace the pink throw pillows with gray concrete slabs? Buy a black collar for Bogey instead of the collar with frolicking lambs and a tinkling bell? Liam loves Lorelei's dog, but even I'd go nuts with the little bell that sometimes graces its neck.

I giggle to myself as I step into Lorelei's kitchen and note the appetizers on trays and bottles of top-shelf liquor. Apparently, Lorelei wants to make an impression tonight.

My eyes move to the stand mixer on the counter. "What can I eat here in my condition?" I ask.

"Uh, stay away from the brownies and the banana bread."

I laugh for real this time, not stifling it. I bend at the waist and grip my thighs as Lorelei impatiently taps her foot near me. "What is so funny?" she asks.

I straighten and hold my hand over my stomach as I wipe my nose. "You're hosting a party for drug task force agents and serving edibles."

She shrugs. "Liam was the biggest holdout, and he's OK with his coworkers having a brownie now. Not that he'd ever do it." She walks to the mixer and inhales deeply. "He still has a stick up his ass about doing it himself."

"Well, at least his coworkers don't have you in cuffs and in the back of a car for a citation," I say, remembering how Liam had it in for her when they met.

"True that," she says. She empties the mixture bowl into a pan while I silently take a seat on a stool at her counter. I watch as she gets another batch of prepared ingredients from the fridge and gently scrapes them into the mixing bowl. She turns the mixer on and faces me. "Now, tell me how he took the news."

"News?"

"Did you decide what you're doing? He looks happy enough, so maybe you're keeping the baby?"

I look down at her counter and trace my fingers around the marble swirls. "Well, it hasn't exactly come up."

Lorelei's eyes bug out of her head, and she slaps my shoulder with the nearby plastic cutting board. "What the fuck, Kailee?" she loudly whispers. "He doesn't know? You guys are getting this close and you still haven't told him?" She wildly points in the direction of the other room.

"It hasn't come up!" I whisper yell back.

Lorelei cringes and shakes her head. "Hasn't come up? Is he just going to ask if you're pregnant out of the blue? This is something the woman kind of has to bring up! He can't read your mind. Are you going to tell him when he's hugging you in a few months and the baby kicks against his stomach?"

"OK, you have a point."

"From the way you're carrying on and the smile on his face when I opened the door, I was about to ask him when the baby shower is. Jesus, Kailee, you have to tell him."

"I still don't know what I'm going to do."

"Well, the countdown clock is kind of winding down on that window. You need to tell him so you can figure it out together. Why am I still telling you this? This has been the only topic of conversation with you lately. Tell him so I know whether I'm planning a baby shower or taking off work to hold your hand at a clinic."

"It's going so well with him. I'm afraid of fucking it up."

"Every single day you keep this from him, you dig yourself further into the hole."

"I know, but it's never the right time," I whine.

"When isn't it the right time? Work it in."

I tap my toes on the linoleum under my seat. "What do you want from me? Was I supposed to tell him while he was fucking me against the wall in the teacher workroom? When he was sucking marmalade off my boobs while working me with his hand? Yeah, I'll just be like, 'Feels good. By the way, you're going to be a dad.' That's not something you tell a man during sex or on a first date."

Heat rises to my face, and Lorelei also blushes. I'm flushed in anger that she won't get off my back about telling him about the baby. She reddens because she's probably picturing the marmalade scene and really doesn't want to see that in her mind.

She blinks twice. "I really don't have an answer for that, but I think your life is vastly more interesting than I give you credit for."

Liam walks into the kitchen at that moment, and we're silent as he walks to the refrigerator and grabs four beers out of the side door. He turns to leave and catches us staring at him. "What's up?"

"How do you feel about marmalade?" Lorelei asks.

"What?" Liam asks.

"Nothing! She means nothing," I say, swiping my hand through the air and connecting with Lorelei's shoulder. "Lorelei thinks she's funny. Nothing to see here. Carry on. Take your beers out. This is woman stuff."

"Woman's stuff?" he asks, a wry grin on his face.

"Yeah, you know. Boys. Makeup. Um…hair accessories," I say.

"I'm out," Liam replies, raising his hands like he's had enough. "I'll be in the other room with the men folk."

"OK, bye," Lorelei and I both say as Liam crinkles his brow but still leaves the room, the swinging door flapping in his wake.

Once he's gone, I whirl on Lorelei. "Please tell me you haven't told Liam about any of this."

Lorelei slides down the counter until she's practically on her knees. "I haven't," she says, drawing out each syllable. "It's killing me." She curls her fingers like she's trying not to claw at her face or hair. "Do you know how hard it is to not tell the love of your life that his best friend is having a baby with your best friend?"

"No, I don't."

"And I hope you never know this feeling."

"I just hoped I'd have more of an idea of what I want to do about it."

Lorelei picks up a nearby rag and then flops it right back down in a huff. "Let him be the tiebreaker then. If you tell him, you'll have more information to make the decision, right?"

"I guess."

"You'll know if he'll be involved and by how much. Will he at least pay child support without you chasing him for eighteen years? If not, you'll know what you need to do. If he will pay support and make sure your child has childcare and college tuition, you'll know you can have it."

I hold up a finger. "Medical issues."

"I know, Kailee, but you need to go to the damn doctor. You're being infuriatingly immature about this. Medical care is very different from thirty years ago. Hell, they didn't schedule cesareans then, and the doctor could do that for you now if she's worried."

"I'm frozen in fear!"

"What will it take to get you unfrozen?"

I blow out a deep breath through my nose. "I don't know. I don't know anything about any of this. I hear myself when I talk, OK? I do. I just...can't stop the onslaught of intrusive thoughts assailing my mind every hour of every day."

Lorelei walks around the counter, her kitten heels she probably wore to show Liam she could be the stereotypical perfect hostess clacking against her black-and-white linoleum. When she's next to me, she puts her arm around me, pulling me so close that I catch a whiff of her body spray. "If you can't decide, you need the advice of someone invested and trustworthy. He's both. You have to let him show you what he's capable of."

Chapter 14

CHASE

She's still here with me. We came to my house together last night and climbed into bed. She's wearing my shirt and a pair of my boxer briefs, and I told her she could bring a few things over if she would stay over more often. She didn't comment or immediately say she'd bring over her tampons and toothpaste, but she didn't run out. She didn't call an Uber. She didn't sneak out from under my arm in the middle of the night. I know because I stayed awake to make sure. We didn't have sex because she was too tired, and I was a bit more inebriated than I should have been, but I held her all night.

She stirs in my arms, and I pull her close to my chest. "Good morning," I whisper into her hair.

She makes an indiscernible sound that sounds like her telling me to go fuck myself, but I'll take any sound she gives me in the morning. Eventually, she must realize where she is, and she reaches back, patting my curls and running her hand down the sandpaper of my morning face.

"Chase?"

"I really hope you're just confirming it's me and not wondering which of your many men is with you."

She laughs, and I'm surprised when she snuggles back into me. Thankfully, she doesn't wiggle her ass or grind against me. A quick look at my alarm clock confirms we'd both be late for work if we linger in bed.

"I don't want this to ever change between us," I whisper, placing small kisses all over her shoulder and neck. "I want you like this. Just us."

She stills for a moment. "Did I say something wrong?" I ask.

She shakes her head. "No, Chase. I like this."

"If I'm rushing you, I'll back off. I just...I'm not seeing anyone else. I don't want to date other women. I'm not saying we'll get married, but I want to see where this goes. I didn't mean to scare you."

She waves her hands in front of her face and gives an awkward smile as she sits up and turns to look at me. "It's fine, Chase. Good."

It doesn't feel good, though. It kind of feels like I stepped in dog shit, and I have no idea why. All I did was tell her I just wanted it to be the two of us.

She huffs in annoyance with what I hope is just the dread of starting her day and swings her legs over the side of the bed. I run my hand up her back once, just to touch her, and marvel at how hot she looks in my borrowed underpants and shirt.

No touch back. She doesn't grab my hand or turn to give me a kiss on the cheek. Nothing.

"We better get going," she mumbles, stumbling her way to my bathroom. She wipes her eyes like she's utterly exhausted, which I don't understand. She had a few hours of sleep. Is she one of those people who get crabby if they don't get ten hours?

***

I'm irritated after five minutes in this place. Some jack nuts drank all the flavored coffee in the coffee pod carousel, and I'm left with light roast. A man can't effectively protect an entire school on light roast. What's next? Decaf? It probably wasn't Leo, but I blame Leo.

It's also bothering me how Kailee acted this morning. I asked in the car if she was OK, and she said she was just tired and groggy with a headache. I didn't see her drink last night, but maybe she had a couple beers when I wasn't looking.

I should take her something. Something she'll appreciate. Something to make her eyes light up.

I'll go get some Jell-O.

I can't get to the store until after my lunch hour and walk through, and when I finally do get to the store at the end of fifth hour, only blue raspberry is left. Maybe she'll like it. Either way, it's what I have.

I knock on the door to her room. I've come in before, and I know that the students mostly work in groups at this point in class. Sauntering in like I own the place, I stop dead when I find Leo Paulson sitting behind the teacher's desk with a scowl on his face.

"What are you doing in here?" he asks in a gruff voice.

"I could ask you the same question," I say, matching his tone.

My words are like a needle scratch on a record. The entire class stops whatever they're doing to stare at me. Electric mixers click off. Knives stop cutting. A few girls inhale deeply, obviously anticipating either Leo or I to pull out swords and fight to the death for Ms. Lipshitz.

Too bad my good sword is in my other pants.

Leo gets out of the chair and crosses the room in four quick strides. He pulls my arm, and I shake him off before he gestures to the corner. Reluctantly, I walk with him. I guess he just wants to tell me why he's in here.

"It's my plan time, so Kailee sent a student over to get me to cover her class," Leo explains, his eyes on my chest. I detect the slightest pectoral flex from him like he's trying to show me he lifts.

"Is she sick?"

He shrugs. "The girl she sent told me she thinks Kailee got her period or something. There were some dots on the back of her pants."

I let out a sigh of relief. She's probably just in the nurse's office getting a tampon and some suitable pants or something. She'll be back in a bit.

"What's in the bag?" Leo asks, nodding toward the plastic grocery bag.

"None of your fucking business," I say a little too loudly, pulling the bag away from him. Thankfully, high school seniors don't even register the word as outside the realm of normal conversation.

"Leave it here for her. I'll make sure she gets it."

I squint at Leo. "Hell no. You'll take credit for it."

"I will not. You're being a baby."

I sneer at him and walk from the room, careful not to slam the door behind me. From outside, I can barely make out Leo throwing his hands up and stomping to the teacher's desk, ignoring a young lady with her hand up as he passes.

I'll go to the nurse's office and make sure she's fine. If she's embarrassed or something about her period, she can tell me to leave. No big deal. But at least I can make sure she gets the Jell-O. I'm not leaving it on her desk where Leo can swipe it into the trash can or take credit for it.

I walk to the nurse's office and tap on the door frame when I enter the room. Kailee is sitting on the exam table with swollen eyes, and the school nurse, Becky, is pulling out the exam table so Kailee can put her feet up.

"Kailee?" I ask, moving further into the room but taking baby steps. "Are you OK? Leo said you came down here for your period or something."

Becky turns and looks between us before looking back at Kailee.

"Why are you crying?" I ask. Why aren't they answering me? "Do you have cramps?" I look at Becky. "Give her some painkiller or something."

"Do you want some ibuprofen?" Becky asks like she's never thought about giving a grown adult in the office for their period actual medicine before. She digs through a drawer in the exam table and holds out a travel pack of something.

Kailee's eyes don't leave mine, and there's something in them...something I don't recognize.

She holds her hand up and gently pushes the offered medicine away. She nods slightly like she's resigning herself to something – like she's stepping up to the plate.

"It's not my period, Chase. I'm eleven weeks pregnant and spotting."

I tilt my head and look at her, trying to understand the words that just came out of her mouth. My brain sputters like an old car with a dying battery sputtering to life while Becky prattles about resting, putting her feet up, and making an appointment with a doctor.

A doctor? Why does Kailee need a doctor?

What does the word pregnant mean?

Pregnant...pregnant...That means a baby is inside of my girlfriend, right? Eleven weeks? Is that a long time? Is that months, years, or days? I've lost the entire concept of time as the world tilts on its axis. Somehow, my body knows something I'm missing because my limbs tense. My toes curl. My balls scrunch up inside my body like I'm naked in a snowstorm.

My mind spins as I connect the dots...*slow* dots.

Saltines.

Nausea.

Cravings.

Exhaustion.

The feeling she harbors a big secret she wants to tell but can't.

Her breasts looking mighty scrumptious, fit for any baby or man to nurse from.

Dear God, I'm the dumbest mother fucker alive.

Who's the father? Wait. We had sex in the workroom a week ago, so that doesn't equal eleven weeks. Her date with Leo wasn't that long ago. That can't be eleven weeks either.

I drop the bag in my hand and brace one hand against the wall, ticking off weeks on my other hand's fingers as I wrack my brain. It's been about three months, give or take, since we met. I don't know for sure. I can't think. I can't count.

Once I finally get back to the realm of time we met on my fingers, I can't breathe.

A familiar feeling I've only felt a few times before moves through my body. The last time I felt it was when I had to kill a drug dealer and bring Liam back from the brink of death. It's terror. Unadulterated fear. My vision tunnels, and I'm glad I'm in a nurse's office in case I go down. My heart pounds so hard that I can't hear anything but the buzz of my pulse.

This can't be happening, but I have to do something. Say something.

Somewhere across space and time, Becky wets a washcloth for the back of Kailee's neck and fills up a cup of water. Seconds tick by as Kailee stares at me, her bottom lip trembling. She looks like a child in the nurse's office for a skinned knee. So vulnerable. So innocent.

She needs me. How long has she known and been dealing with this?

I open my mouth to talk, to tell her we'll get through it, but words don't come out. I squeeze the door because my knees buckle under me, and this flimsy taxpayer-purchased wood is the only thing keeping me upright.

Becky says something about the baseball playoffs and wearing red to support St. Louis next Friday, but I don't care. I don't know if I'll ever care about anything mundane again. Kailee sure doesn't care about baseball because a tear trickles out of her eye, and she doesn't stop staring at me. She waits in silence for me to say something as Becky prattles on, completely oblivious to something else happening in the room.

That something else is my life imploding and Kailee pleading with her eyes that I do something to acknowledge it.

"I can't handle this," I whisper before I sprint from the room on shaky knees, holding on to the wall in the hallway for balance until I push open the double doors to the parking lot and let fresh air fill my lungs.

Chapter 15

KAILEE

Liam squints from the other side of the room, his legs crossed so that his ankle is over the other knee. "Let me understand this. You're pregnant?" he asks, pointing at my stomach. "And Chase is the father. My Chase?" I nod. "You guys hooked up at the bar that night." He turns his head and looks at the carpet. "I knew it!"

I sniff and wipe my nose on my sleeve as Lorelei pops back into the room with a cup of weak tea to help my stomach. I haven't seen Chase since he ran from the nurse's office yesterday. I didn't want to be alone, so I found myself over at Lorelei's for a shoulder to cry on. Per usual, Liam is here and even opened the door to find my crying ass on the doorstep. I still don't know why he hasn't moved in yet. I kind of had to tell him what happened.

Lorelei sets the teacup in front of me and intentionally avoids her boyfriend's eyes. "Yes, it's Chase's baby. Can we move past that and deal with the issue at hand?"

"How long have you known?" Liam asks.

"I've known for a couple weeks. I just couldn't tell him," I say.

"Not you." He points at Lorelei this time. "You. How long did you know about this and not fill me in?"

Lorelei bites her lip. "Umm. I don't remember."

"Bullshit."

Lorelei rolls her shoulders. These two have been all over each other for months now, and it's almost good to see them back to the angry banter they had when they met. They square off against each other well. You'll never convince me otherwise.

"It wasn't my story to tell, *Liam*."

Liam leans forward. "But that story is about my best friend and partner, *Lorelei*."

Lorelei scowls and leans forward, not breaking his eye contact now. "And she's *my* best friend –

"Just stop it," I interrupt, putting my hands out like I'll need to push them apart. "You both sound ridiculous. This isn't high school where everyone needs to gossip. I told her not to tell anyone because I still don't know what I'm going to do." I glare at Liam. "She'd keep any secret you have."

That fact seems to placate him as his jaw relaxes, and he finally leans back against Lorelei's pink throw pillows. Lorelei turns her attention back to me and runs her hand down my back. "What did he say?"

"He said he couldn't handle it."

"What?" They both yell the word at the same time. They look at each other, and Lorelei grits her teeth. Liam shrugs, but his lip curls.

"What do you mean he said he couldn't handle it?" Lorelei asks.

"I didn't get a chance to clarify because he literally ran from the room. I watched him through the little window in the door. It was like Usain Bolt realized he had to be anywhere but in that nurse's office. I've never seen a man run so fast." I look at Liam. "Did he run track?"

Liam shrugs. "News to me. He batted before me in the work softball league last year, and I practically had to pick him up and carry him around the bases when I hit a home run. I'd classify his run as more of a jaunty jog."

"So this is just a 'I found out I'm going to be a father' thing?"

Liam sighs and shakes his head, a confused look creasing his brow. "I hope not. It just doesn't sound like him. He's always been able to handle anything thrown at him. We've been on some undercover busts, and even when we were almost found out, he stayed calm and in character. He doesn't punk out on stakeouts, and a few weeks ago wasn't the first time he saved my life. It was the most intense, but not the first. He handles problems quickly. I mean, you can't be a drug task force agent and not be able to take some shit, you know?"

"Why did he run then?" Lorelei asks.

"Shock?" Liam suggests. "Maybe he just needed air?"

"Must have been suffocating," I mumble. A tear courses down my cheek, and I don't wipe it. I let it drip to Lorelei's carpet. She reaches for a nearby box of tissues and hands me one before thinking better of it and handing me the entire box.

I accept the box and blow my nose. "I was spotting and –

"Are you still spotting?" Lorelei interrupts. Her eyes flick to the white and pink couch under me like she's worried about a stain. I know she's more worried about me, so her look is probably a reflex.

"Not much. It's mostly just..." I trail off and look at Liam. I'm not sure he can handle spotting talk. Then again, he just said drug task force agents deal with a lot of shit. He can probably handle vaginal bleeding. "It's just spotty and dark. Not bright red."

Lorelei blows out a breath. "I think you should go to the doctor. Finally."

"I made an appointment for tomorrow. I also read up on it last night because I couldn't sleep, and there's not much they can do at this point anyway, but I should probably see a doctor."

A knock on the front door startles all of us, and I freeze. Chase? The Amazon delivery guy? Oh, please let it be the delivery guy. I'm not sure if I could face Chase looking at me again and hoofing it back to his car.

Lorelei gets up slowly and practically tiptoes to the door, probably knowing exactly what I'm thinking. When she looks out the peephole, she chuckles and flings the door open.

"Mom?" Liam asks as Nola Lane comes through the door.

She pauses to hug Lorelei and shoves a Tupperware dish of something at her. Nola and Lorelei are always exchanging food. Nola cooks savory meals that are so mouth-wateringly good they'll make you come. Lorelei bakes and provides edibles to Nola as she recovers from her chemo treatments. Nola hasn't had chemo for a few weeks, and she's getting her energy back.

I nod at Nola as she shuffles into the room. Liam stands to hug her. "What are you doing here?"

Nola waves her hand as she sits in the extra reclining chair next to the sofa. "Ah, I made some pork loin and potatoes I thought Lorelei would like."

"You didn't think I'd like it, Mom?"

"Pfft." She ignores her son, and Liam shakes his head. Lorelei and Nola are so close now that it's almost comical how Liam feels left out.

Nola slaps her thighs and looks around the room. "How have you been, Kailee?"

"Just fine, ma'am."

Lorelei comes back into the room and hands me a bottle of ginger ale.

"Oh, you're pregnant, huh?" Nola asks.

I blink and freeze. "I beg your pardon?"

Nola points to the ginger ale. "I downed that by the case when I was pregnant with Liam. The only other time I drank it was during chemo, and I think someone would have told me if you're getting chemo."

Lorelei and Liam don't answer. Lorelei sits on her sofa next to Liam and takes his hand. I decide to answer honestly. "Yes, ma'am. I'm here because your son's partner knocked me up when I was bent over his kitchen counter, and now I don't know what to do."

Nola nods. "It happens. Gotta say that I'm impressed you banged Officer Handsome. That man is one good-looking hombre. Kitchen counter, you say?"

"Mom," Liam groans.

I sit a little straighter. Maybe this is who I need to talk to. "Hey, you had Liam on your own and raised him as a single mother. If you had to do it all over again, would you?"

Nola smiles and looks at the ceiling like she's trying to re-member. "Well, first off, his father was with me when I had him. He didn't come into the room because he was weird about that, but he was at the hospital. He left a couple days later and didn't look back." Nola looks at Liam pointedly. "If he had taken off before that, I don't know what I would have done, to be honest. I was still recovering when Liam's dad did a runner, and we hadn't filed the birth certificate yet. I put my last name on it instead of his. That was my way of being mad."

"Understandable, Mom."

"Did you know he would leave you?" I shake my head. "Sorry. I'm just really trying to work out if I should have this baby or not. I can't do it on my own. From what I understand, you had a good job as a nurse."

"Yep. Robert, that's Liam's father, also left me enough money to get by for a while. He had a pretty successful drywall and remodeling business, and he was generous with me. We'd been together off and on since I was eighteen when we were paired for a dance contest in Chicago, but there was a lot I didn't know about him."

"A dance contest?" I ask, arching an eyebrow.

"Long story."

"You never told me that," Liam says.

"We won, too. Well, co-won. We tied with another pair. Anyway, we were around thirty when I got pregnant, and I had been a nurse for a few years by then. It was a good job. After he ran his errand, I found a sizable check in an envelope. My mother watched Liam before he started school so I was able to work without daycare cost. I'm one of the lucky ones, though. If he hadn't left that money and I hadn't had help from my family, I don't know what I would have done. I would have definitely been on assistance, even with my job. Daycare cost is no joke, even back in the late last century."

"You never looked for him?" I ask.

"Nope. I didn't feel like chasing someone who didn't want to be with me. I had a kid to look after. I knew that he wouldn't be a good dad to Liam if he didn't want to be here. Did I mention the check was enough to supplement my job for a long time? Why blow it on a lawyer to get the child support I may or may not have been able to count on?"

She looks at the floor. "I never heard from him again. He was from the Chicago area, so I assume he went back there. He probably had a family at some point. He just didn't want one with me. We were together off and on for several years, and when I look back, I realize there were clues I missed."

"Like what?" I ask, scooting to the edge of my seat. When Nola talks, it's always profound. At least, that's what Lorelei says. Liam also scoots forward, his ear turned toward his mother. Has he never asked this before?

She cocks her head and taps her chin. "Little things. He missed Chicago. He'd wax poetic about it. I knew he had a wandering eye, and part of me wondered if there was a girlfriend up there that happened one of the times we were off and he just didn't tell me she existed when we got back together. He'd visit Chicago a lot. Hell, I could have been the other woman. In the end, he spent more time up there than down here, but I didn't think much about it. His drywall business was all over Illinois, Missouri, and Iowa. Was he married to someone else? Did he have a woman who was in the same situation, and he had to choose between us? He was nervous all the time during my pregnancy, but I chalked it up to him being scared of fatherhood. Looking back, I'm almost certain something was going on up there." She looks behind me like she's lost in memory. "Whatever the case, you can't force someone to love you because you have a child together."

"But did you regret it?" I ask, desperate to know from someone with hindsight. A tear leaks out of my left eye, and I reach for another tissue. I look at Lorelei, who is red in the face and scowling, her fists balled in anger at my situation or Liam being left by his father. Maybe both.

Nola looks at me and then moves her eyes to my stomach. "No." She waves her hand up and down Liam. "I mean, look at what I did. I raised this. It wasn't always easy, and I had it pretty darn easy compared to some."

"What would you have done if it wasn't easy? If you were alone and without a big cash infusion and no job with benefits? Because that's what I'm dealing with if Chase wants to keep running until he reaches the Canadian border."

She clucks and shakes her head. "If I was in that situation, I don't know. I wonder about women in that situation every day." She shrugs. "Especially in the current climate. But I love this guy, and we got through it by the skin of our teeth with lots of help. I sure can empathize with women who don't have any means or help, though. I think the entire world could do with a bit of empathy for each woman's situation and stop trying to paint such a sensitive and private subject for each individual woman with a broad brush. Forced poverty isn't good for anyone."

Liam clears his throat and runs his hand through his dark hair, ruffling it a bit. "But in all seriousness, I think Chase will come around," he says. "He's not like my dad. He won't leave you to fend for yourself. He doesn't have a secret wife or girlfriend. I can assure you of that. He's all about you."

"You can't be sure of that."

Liam leans forward and cryptically looks out the window as Lorelei practically trembles with rage next to him. "Yes, I damn well can." He drops Lorelei's hand. "I have to run an errand."

"Maybe he is a little like his dad," Nola mumbles after Liam stomps from the house, letting the door slam shut behind him.

Chapter 16

CHASE

I swing the door open and frown when I find a red-in-the-face Liam on my front porch, his eyes wide and his lips a tight line. He briefly eyes my loose bathrobe and my mussed hair before squinting and shaking his head like I've shocked him with my disheveled appearance. "Prepare to defend yourself, mother fucker."

I step back, and it's my turn to be confused. "What?" I ask, running my hand down day-old scruff.

"Let's go," he says with a shrug. "We have business."

"I can't deal with any work shit now. I've had a rough couple of days."

"This is personal." Liam gestures to my yard. "Outside. Now."

I look behind me like there may be someone in my living room that he's talking to. When I face him again, I find him tapping his foot, his jaw set.

"What is this?" I ask again. "Why are you pissed at me?"

"I'm here to kick your ass into next Tuesday." He holds up his hands. "Don't get me wrong. I still owe you for saving my life, you're my best friend, and you're my partner who's always had my back. But I have to kick your ass because you did a shitty thing to my girl's best friend, and if I don't kick your ass, I'm going to have to explain why I didn't beat the shit out of you to Lorelei. It was either me coming to handle business or she was going to come over and disconnect your balls from your body." He makes a come here motion with his fingers. "Just take your pounding so I can tell her it's done and she won't hurt either of us."

"Should I be scared of her?"

"Terrified, man. She will *take* your balls."

"She's taken yours," I mumble, bracing my arms on my doorframe.

Liam turns his head like he wants me to speak louder. "What the fuck did you say?"

"Nothing, nothing. I didn't say anything about your new girlfriend carrying your balls around in her purse." I take two steps off my front porch. "Alright. Let's get this over with. I deserve it."

"You know you did a shitty thing?" Liam asks, putting his fists up like we're going to box.

"Yeah," I say. I look around at the grass and nod. "What I did was shitty, and I don't know how to fix it. I was shocked, to say the least. Go ahead and hit me. Hell, man, pound me into the dirt."

"You're taking the fun right out of this." He raises his fists again and steps toward me. "Where do you want it?"

"Thank you for asking me what part of my face I want you to fuck up. Very charitable of you." I sigh and point to my chin. "Here, but don't bust any teeth because I want veneers, and it will be a good chance to make you pay for them. Since we're best friends, I feel like I should tell you that."

Liam gives a short nod and then swings. I squint before his fist connects with my chin, but not looking at him when he throws a punch doesn't dull the pain that floods my face. My jaw clicks, and I move it around for a second to make sure it's not broken as I stumble into my mailbox.

"What the fuck? You actually hit me!" I yell, spit dripping out of my mouth because I really wasn't ready for the punch.

"I wasn't fucking kidding!" he yells back.

He offers me his hand to help me stand upright, but I slap it away. "Fuck off. I'm going through some shit right now, and my best friend comes over and hits me?"

"I warned you first and asked you where you wanted it! You think I was going to give you a love tap? And why the fuck is

Kailee at my house right now and crying about you getting her pregnant and acting like a complete shithead?"

"Because I got her pregnant and then acted like a complete shithead!" I yell.

The neighbor across the street, Edna Glasgow, opens her screen door. She's carrying her little, white dog, and she shuffles onto her porch, adjusting her glasses and holding an old flip phone from the turn of the century. I wave at her and turn Liam so he sees we have an audience.

He gives an awkward wave when he sees her on the porch. "Good afternoon, ma'am," he says. He gestures between us. "Just having a conversation with Chase."

"I saw you hit that young man!" she yells with a shaky voice from across the street. She crooks a gnarled finger at Liam and shakes it. "I'm going to call the police on you."

Liam reaches into his back pocket and pulls out his badge. He casually flips it open. "I am the police, ma'am." He points to me. "He is, too. He's just acting like an idiot, so I had to knock some sense into him. Partner stuff. You understand?"

"Partner stuff, huh?" She sniffs and clutches her dog closer. "Didn't know he was like that. He doesn't put that rainbow flag out in June or anything."

"Shit," I whisper under my breath. I pinch my nose in irritation and immediately grunt from the pain. My whole face hurts.

"You don't be abusive to your partner, now. I don't care which way your bologna is buttered. I know the rate of domestic violence with police officers and their lovers. I saw it on the news." Edna wags her fingers at Liam like she's scolding a toddler. "You watch it, son. If there's a bruise on him, I'll call your superior."

She backs into her house and glares at us from behind the screen door as Liam and I stare at her.

I don't know what to say to the fact that Liam and I were just accused of being two gay police officers involved in a violent domestic dispute, and Liam's silence tells me he doesn't either. Finally, I blow Edna a kiss. "Thank you, queen! You've always been my favorite neighbor."

"What the fuck are you doing?" Liam asks under his breath, his eyes wide and staring at the lawn near his feet.

"That was nice of her to look out for me like that. Maybe you'll think twice about hitting me again. And there's nothing wrong with being in love with me, Liam. You could do worse. Hell, we used to pick up women together. You *have* done worse. Lorelei excluded."

"Get in the house so we can talk without neighbor interruption."

I hold up my hands and walk back to the door. "Fine. You're the one who called me to the front yard anyway."

I march into the house and cringe at the sight of my own filth. Liam's never seen my house like this, and he gasps behind me as he steps through the door.

Two pizza boxes are on the floor, pistachio ice cream drips down the paper container onto my coffee table, and three beer cans are on their sides on my couch. Tissues are everywhere. This place either looks like a woman was just dumped and then watched *Beaches* on repeat or a teenage boy ran out of socks.

"Have you been crying?"

I put my hands on my hips and jut out my freshly bruised chin. "Wouldn't you?"

"If I found out I was going to be a father? No."

"Just out of curiosity, what would your reaction be if Lorelei told you she's pregnant?" I ask.

He smiles a wry grin and flushes. "I would pick her up and kiss every inch I could reach. I would run around the room crying tears of joy and then probably go over to my work lover's house with cigars and a bottle of whiskey."

I throw a pillow at him and plop on my couch. He sits in the leather chair across from me and props his chin in his hands. "Why did you react that way?" he asks.

"I'm scared, Liam. It was like an out-of-body experience. I've been shot at, almost lost you, and we've dealt with some bad mother fuckers, but I've never felt as shocked and scared as I did when she said she's pregnant. I was literally floating above my body and watching everything. I waited while my brain tried to catch up with my balls because my balls immediately knew something was wrong, but I couldn't handle it. I was still frozen in so much fear that I opened my mouth and said stupid shit.

Then, my legs wanted to run, and I'm not just talking about going for a jog. They wanted away. I felt like I could run a marathon just from fear."

"So, you left her there without saying a fucking word?"

"I think I said I couldn't handle it." I look at Liam, pleading. "But I didn't mean the baby. I meant the conversation right then, but my brain..." I trail off and wave my hand near my head. "My brain shut down, and all my words came out wrong." I inhale a deep breath. "Is she OK? Is she still bleeding?"

"It's stopped. She seems to be OK. No pain and no more blood." He looks around the room and wipes his face. "You have to fix this."

I lean back and cross my arms over my chest. "I know, but I don't want to fuck it up again." I look at my feet propped on my coffee table. "She's pretty upset, huh?"

Liam tilts his head, studying me. "Can you handle the baby?"

"I don't know, and I don't know if she wants me to."

"Are you going to be there for her?"

I grit my teeth. "What in our friendship would make you think I would leave her to this by herself? But she'd have to let me help, Liam. Fuck, I've done nothing but want to be with her since I met her. She ran out on me after we fucked – after I got her pregnant, I guess – and now I'm wondering if she's only been nice to me the last couple of weeks because she felt guilty and needed to tell me she's carrying my baby. I'd like to sit and talk with her about it. I've tried texting her a hundred times today but pussed out every time. Would she even talk to me?"

"Want my advice?" he asks.

"What? No more ass kicking?"

He shakes his head and smirks. "I'd never do anything to hurt you, sweetheart." I glare at him, and his smile slides off his face. "You need to fix it, and you need to find your balls. Those are the hairy things under your dick."

"My balls are smooth and pretty," I whisper. I idly pick up my melting ice cream and swish green liquid around the container as I think. "The thing is, Liam, I'm scared."

"I know. It's a big deal to become someone's father."

"But I'd suck it up for her. Want to know why I'm scared?"

"Tell me."

"Because I'm powerless. It's like being put into a runaway train car, and you're not sure whether to do a tuck and roll out the caboose or hold on tight and hope everything turns out OK."

"Funny that you've figured out this father thing already."

"I can't do anything for her right now, you know? No matter what I think or feel, she's the one who is sick and scared and going to have to push something the size of a watermelon out of something the width of the average churro, and I don't know the right thing to say to support her."

"How about, 'Hey, Kailee. I'm here.' Then, you hug her tight, stroke her hair, and tell her you'll support whatever choice she makes." He stops and stares at the wall behind me, probably thinking of more advice. "You should also throw in a forehead kiss. Women love those."

"I would do all those things for her. But then I'll wait on pins and needles to see what she decides."

Liam wipes his forehead like he's annoyed at me. He leans back and stretches his long legs out on my coffee table. "So wait on pins and needles until she tells you what to do. But you need to apologize first and tell her you will wait for her direction."

"I know. I'll tell her at work tomorrow."

"She won't be there."

I lift my head. "Did she quit?"

Liam coughs out a laugh. "Yeah, a single pregnant woman is going to quit the job she needs." He shakes his head. "She's got a doctor's appointment. She needed one anyway, so she's going tomorrow."

I look at the floor again and chew on my cheek, thinking. "Where's the doctor's appointment?"

Chapter 17

KAILEE

Apparently, there are two types of magazines in gynecology offices. One type is the typical magazine appealing to women in their early twenties with advice on getting a man and giving him great orgasms. On the flipside, the other option is a flock of parenting magazines with pictures of babies wrapped in bath towels. I never thought I'd say it, but I could go for a *Time* or a *US News and World Report* about right now. None of the options on the shelf appeal to a woman in her early thirties who knows her way around a dick but isn't sure she'd make a great mom.

I stick out an index finger toward one of the magazines with a newborn yawning on the cover like I'll be electrocuted if I touch it. I need something to read, though. The doctor is running fifteen minutes late.

I take a deep breath and resign myself to just grabbing it off the magazine rack when a dark shadow looms over me. Turning to see why a stranger in a doctor's office would want to be right against me, my eyes only meet toned pectorals in a gray t-shirt. The familiar hint of laundry soap and cedar fills my nose, and my eyes momentarily flutter as my brain recognizes it. Moments later, I slowly tilt my head to look into the eyes I know well enough by now.

"What the holy hell are you doing here?" I whisper, the magazine rack forgotten. I put my hand out and lean against the beige wall, steadying myself.

Chase purses his lips for a moment and then nods like he's talking himself into something. "Liam told me you have an appointment. I want to be here for you. Is that OK?"

I blink and shake my head a bit, trying to understand. "You want to be here? Why?"

"Because I wasn't the other day, and I feel awful about it. I didn't mean I couldn't handle the baby, Kailee." He runs his hand up my arm, and I tremble with the excitement of his touch. His proximity. He's *here*. "I was shocked and meant I couldn't handle talking about it right then." He closes his eyes and inhales through his nose. "I know you'll be pissed I ask this, but I just need to make sure. It's mine, right?"

"Yes," I say. "And I'm not pissed. It's a legitimate question."

He looks around the room to see if our conversation has drawn attention. Only a middle-aged woman is across the room and reading a paperback. She isn't paying one bit of attention to us.

"Why didn't you tell me?" His forehead crinkles in concern, and my heart breaks into a billion pieces.

"I –

"Kailee Lipshitz?" a nurse asks. She holds an iPad and looks between me and the middle-aged woman.

My hand immediately shoots into the air like I'm in school. "Right here."

"Come on back and bring your...partner?" At least the woman didn't automatically assume that Chase is my husband. That would have made an already awkward moment even more embarrassing.

I follow the nurse and realize Chase isn't behind me when I reach the door to the inner sanctum of the office. "Are you coming?" I ask.

Chase shoves his hands into the pockets of his dark jeans. His shoulders slouch. "Do you want me there?"

I hesitate because I don't want to seem too eager. I grip the doorknob as the nurse stands next to me, patiently understanding that something is happening. She doesn't rush us. I almost hug her for understanding.

"I want you here, Chase. I'm scared. Will you please come with me?"

Maybe it's the look of fear on my face. Maybe he just really cares about me. Maybe it's both. But Chase Barnett flexes his jaw and straightens his shoulders. He walks to the door and cups my face before pushing his nose to mine. "I'm sorry I wasn't here for you the last couple of days. But I'll be here for every doctor's appointment from now on. Understand?"

I nod, my eyes the size of dinner plates at his voice's firmness. He's never talked to me like this before. It must be his police voice – the voice he uses to tell people to drop their weapons and put their hands in the air. I almost go to the wall and spread my legs so he can frisk me. There's something so comforting that he's taking control now.

The nurse clears her throat, bringing us out of our little world. She waves at us to follow her until she takes me to a scale. I hand Chase my purse and step onto it as the nurse writes down my weight, which is two pounds less than what I usually weigh. I'm sure the nausea hasn't helped my body.

I follow the nurse to a small exam room, and she waves me onto the exam table and points to a chair for Chase to sit in as the nurse gathers my vitals like blood pressure, pulse, oxygen level, and asks me all manner of embarrassing questions that I answer honestly, even though I worry what Chase will think. My blood pressure is a little on the low side, and we discuss that. My pulse is a bit fast, and it's probably a result of not eating much. Yes, I have endometriosis. Chase hangs his head and stares at the floor when I confirm I'm not on birth control, and we didn't use a condom. My periods are always irregular. I don't track them. I didn't think I could have kids. I've never had a sexually transmitted disease or been pregnant before. I confirm the date of my last pap smear.

I shake and tremble the whole time.

The nurse whisks from the room after she directs me to get undressed except for my socks and gives me a small gown to change into behind a thin curtain that separates me from Chase. He doesn't invade my privacy or try to peek. He periodically cracks his knuckles from nerves but is otherwise quiet.

I hate the silence between us. "Sorry you had to hear the entire history of my vagina," I whisper from the other side of the curtain as I dangle my legs over the high exam table.

"It was nice to be formally introduced."

I snort a laugh. "Feel free to tell me any embarrassing bumps or secretions from your balls from now on. I just want to make it even."

"Sometimes I get a bit of razor burn when I manscape."

"Are you scared, Chase?"

"I'm petrified, but I know you are too, so I have a lot of catching up to do on the fear."

"Are you only here because Liam told you to be?" I have to know.

He sniffs a little and stands. Tentatively, half his face appears around the curtain, and he stares at me for a second, his expression kind. "I asked him where it was and what time. I'm here on my own volition. We should –

"Hello," Dr. Dewson says as the door swings open. "Oh, who do we have here?" she asks, opening the curtain.

"This is Chase. He's the father."

"I see." She sits in the seat by the computer and logs in to my chart. She hums a bit as she looks over my reason for being here and my medical history. "So, we're having a baby, huh?"

"Apparently."

She nods and glances at our faces. "I'm assuming this was a surprise."

"Yes, ma'am," I whisper.

"A big one," Chase says.

Dr. Dewson blows out a breath and fully swivels the chair to face me. She respectfully looks into my eyes and somehow manages to bring the room into total calm with her posture. "What are we thinking?"

"We don't know," I say.

Chase stiffens and looks between me and the doctor, but he doesn't say anything.

Dr. Dewson gives a curt nod and then stands. She walks over to the sink and quickly washes her hands before reaching for gloves. "Let's take a look and see where we're at so I can give you any information and answer questions that may be able to help. You're spotting?"

"Yes."

"How much?"

Chase quickly sits behind the curtain again as the doctor positions me in the stirrups and squirts lube on her fingers. She inserts her fingers and presses on my stomach in a manner that makes me wonder where she went to medical school. Is this normal procedure? My eyes flick to the curtain, thankful Chase isn't watching me get a pelvic exam. I squeeze my eyes shut as I think about the doctor's question. "Um, just the one day. It was like a light day of my period."

She removes her hand and pulls off her gloves. She puts a paper over my crotch area, and she whips the curtain open to reveal a startled Chase. His eyes bounce around the room like he doesn't know where to look.

"Any nausea?" Dr. Dewson asks, sitting down again.

"Just a couple of times until about the ninth week." Look at me tracking my symptoms properly. If I wasn't so tired, hungry, and scared, I'd be proud of myself. "It's been all the time the last couple of weeks, though. I can only keep down..." My voice trails off, and I look at Chase, then away again. "Peanut butter."

Chase smirks and reddens, looking at his feet.

"I can send you home with some meds to control it enough for you to get something in your system. If you have problems going forward, you need to call me so I can help. I can't help with everything, but I can with that."

"OK," I say, nodding.

"We're going to do an internal ultrasound. I want to see how the baby's moving. Would Dad like to watch?"

"Uh..." His voice trails off, and he looks at me. He leans closer to the exam table. "Would I like to watch?"

"You can." I don't want to deny him anything since he's here.

Dr. Dewson removes a wand-like structure from a nearby machine that I thought was a heart monitor. Then, she opens a condom and rolls it over the wand as I watch in utter horror. Apparently, this is a sex toy machine.

"Is that a dildo machine?" I ask before I can think better of it.

Chase is also eyeing it like he's not sure whether to pick me up and run out of the room or stay and watch my gynecologist shove a condom-wrapped sex toy up my lady area.

"I get that a lot, but no. It's a transvaginal ultrasound. It's how we do ultrasounds in early pregnancy, although you're almost at the point of your first external one. I don't have that equipment here. It's something you schedule downstairs. I'll only be a minute."

I nod and let her lube up the wand. I hardly even notice when my hand is suddenly full of a masculine one, a thumb stroking circles on my palm.

Dr. Dewson slides the wand inside of me and swivels the screen toward us so I can see the black and white blurs on the screen as she adjusts the picture and moves the wand around, trying to capture a picture on the screen.

Eventually, a small blip that looks like an average jellybean comes into focus. It looks like a little blur as it bounces just a bit and something that looks like a pencil eraser pulses. Chase and I freeze, and Chase moves closer to the screen, squinting. "Is that it?"

"That's it. I'd say about eleven and a half weeks from the size and look."

She presses a button on the machine and some pictures spit out onto a small tray. I didn't even think about getting pictures of the baby at this point.

She quickly removes the wand and instructs me to scoot up the table. I hand her the paper covering the top of my crotch and abdomen and quickly adjust my gown. "Why did I spot?" I ask, out of breath.

Maybe it's seeing the baby, but it somehow makes this all a lot more terrifying. My heart pounds. My armpits feel uncomfortably warm, and a drop of sweat rolls down my temple. "Is this because I drank, had sex, and...had sex?" I ask. If Dr. Dewson thinks I'm insane, she doesn't show it. Perhaps she sees lots of single, broke women in her office pulling their hair out and wailing against the fact that they don't want their baby but also *really* want their baby.

She holds up her hands. "No, Kailee. A lot of women don't realize they're even pregnant until seven or eight weeks. They continued with life. Sex is definitely fine and enjoyed up until delivery in a healthy pregnancy. It can cause a bit of spotting, so it could happen again, but some spotting can be normal." She goes back to the computer and scrolls through my chart again.

"At your last checkup, you said you only drink a couple cocktails a week socially. Has that changed?"

"No," I practically whisper.

"As long as you weren't binge drinking every weekend, you've nothing to worry about an occasional couple glasses of wine the last few weeks."

"I, uh, work at a weed truck that serves brownies and...stuff." I sniff and wipe my face, and Chase's hand runs down my back. "We often eat the leftovers or sample while we bake."

Dr. Dewson tilts her head to the side. "Did you stop when you found out you were pregnant?"

"Yes. I wasn't sure I'd keep it, but I stopped just in case."

Chase's head turns to me, tilting, and his brow furrows. If he has questions about my abortion thoughts, now isn't the time for that very necessary conversation.

"Same directions," Dr. Dewson says. "Try not to fret about it. Baby's heart sounds good, and it's moving. Growth is comparable for a baby of that gestational age. We'll just move forward."

"Does the hospital take my insurance?" I hate that I ask the question, but I need to know if medical bankruptcy is going to be a real thing in my life.

Dr. Dewson checks my chart again and squints. "The Affordable Care Act covers the maternity checkups. Everyone gets that. Your insurance has to cover a few things, but there could be a copay for hospital visits, and many plans don't cover the doctor on call or anything like an epidural. The anesthesiologist's bill is separate. It could be several thousand dollars, but you'll have to talk to your insurance company."

I take in a deep breath, and my eyes bug out of my head. I can't afford to give birth in my own damn country. I have nothing.

"Is any specialist covered by my insurance?"

"The lactation consultant, and you get a free breast pump."

"Oh, well, happy day."

"Handled. Don't you worry about any of it, OK," Chase whispers into my ear, smoothing my hair back. I watch Dr. Dewson as she practically swoons over Chase's words. I'd like to, but I'm too worried about being indebted to him.

"Can I exercise and...stuff?" I ask, changing the subject. I'll cry over the medical bill issue later. I also don't want to have sex right at this moment, but it would be nice to know I could in the next few months.

That's if Chase ever wants to touch me again.

Wait. Why am I so concerned about sex with him when he acted the way he did? The thought moves through my head, but I quickly push it away. I'm not sure I'll keep this baby, let alone keep the man who sired it and then acted like a dick by running away when I told him I'm pregnant.

Dr. Dewson smiles and nods. "I can't see any cause for concern with this, Kailee. You have an active fetus, and your uterus feels as expected. We'll get some blood work to check your hormone levels, and I'm sending you home with some prenatal vitamins you need to take while you consider your next move. Activity and even sex are fine as long as you're not actively spotting. I'd wait a few days for right now, though."

"What about my endometriosis? Will that make things harder?"

"I'm not going to lie. You'll have to keep your appointments. Every single one. After we get to the third trimester, you'll be classified as high risk for early delivery and watched closely for preeclampsia."

"Pre what?"

"High blood pressure. Endometriosis can also cause early delivery. Do not be one of those pregnant women who plans a vacation to Tahiti in their thirty-eighth week. We'll watch you closely when you get there. However, everything looks OK now, and women with endometriosis history deliver full-term, healthy babies all the time once they do get pregnant. If the baby is sticking, we'll roll with it. If baby decides to unstick in the next few weeks, you'll need an office visit, but there's nothing we can do to stop a natural miscarriage at this point. Basically, it is what it is, and right now, it's growing quite nicely."

We all sit in silence for a few moments. I wish I could open a flap into Chase's mind to figure out what in the world is going through his head right now. He's had much less time to adjust to this. I'm sure his head is spinning with questions for me.

Something tells me it will be a long day with some discussion I've been putting off.

Dr. Dewson stands and hands me a packet. "Here is some information about your stage of pregnancy." She picks up the pictures from the tray. "These are yours. I know you have some tough decisions, and I've included information about those choices in the back of the packet. I can't give you more information because the state of Missouri and the Catholic hospital system I'm associated with forbids me even talking about it and have tied doctors' hands, but I can point you to this number here." I look at the number she taps with her index finger way down at the bottom of the page under a bunch of religious-affiliated birth and pregnancy centers. "You understand?"

"Yes, ma'am."

"You have a prescription for prenatal vitamins, and you need to schedule your sixteen-week appointment and ultrasound for twelve weeks at the desk before you leave. I already sent the orders. Go ahead and schedule. You can always cancel if you decide not to go through with the pregnancy. Call the nurse line if you have any questions, OK?"

I nod as she pats Chase on the arm before leaving the room.

I dress in silence behind the curtain as Chase paces on the other side. I can see his outline as I pull up my panties and fasten my bra. He runs his hands through his hair and shakes his head, nods, then shakes it again.

I open the curtain and walk out of the room with him behind me, and we're silent as we head to the front scheduling area. I make appointments as Chase opens his phone and updates his calendar with the dates I work out with the scheduler. He doesn't fuss if he has something scheduled those days. He simply adds them to his phone without expression.

When we're out of the office and standing in front of my car, he finally speaks. "I have to go into a counseling session with the police counselor about the shooting, and then I have a meeting about some cases they want Liam and me to work on when I'm back in the bullpen. I want to talk about this, though. Can we take a few moments over the next couple of days to think and then talk?"

I nod and walk to my car, a tear already threatening to run down my cheek. When will this crying ever stop? "I think that would be good. Um, do you mean where we are with each other or where we are with the baby?"

Chase looks at the keys now in his hand. "Both."

I nod. Chase walks to his car without hugging me, and I bite my lip. I will not let him go like that. Hell no.

"Chase! Wait." I jog over to him, and he steps toward me, his head cocked to the side. When I reach him, I throw my arms around his body, hoping and praying he hugs me back.

I practically swoon with relief when he wraps his arms around me and kisses the top of my head. His arms are so tight around me that I can hardly breathe, but I revel in the feel of his chest against my cheek as he takes a breath – like that will be enough for us. His face is in my hair, and I rub his lower back as he holds me.

I've never felt so safe. So cared for. So much like this is going to be OK whatever we decide. I just hate the feeling that he's holding me like this only because of the baby. The thought gnaws into my soul like an emotional party pooper. Whatever I feel with him, however safe he makes me feel, I cannot get into a relationship with him *just* because we have a child together.

A car honks at us, and we break our hug as we realize we're standing in the middle of the parking lot and blocking traffic. When we move out of the way, Chase kisses me gently on the cheek, and I suddenly remember I'm holding a packet of baby stuff. "Here," I say. I pull out the folder Dr. Dewson gave me and ruffle through it until I find one of the pictures. "You should have one of these."

Chase smiles and takes it from me before finally backing away and looking at his watch. "We'll talk soon, Kailee."

Chapter 18

KAILEE

I expect the knock at my door, but I startle as the sound echoes through my apartment. I drop the spoon I had just pulled out of a drawer, and it falls to the counter with a clatter as a yelp comes from my mouth. I cover my mouth with both hands.

"Kailee?" Chase's voice asks from the other side of the door. I quickly open the door and allow him to cup my face and bend to my eye level. "You OK? I heard a noise when I knocked."

I push his hands down. "Relax. You just startled me. You have that police knock thing down."

"Sorry. Habit."

"Come on in." I open the door wider and let his body touch mine as he slides past me on the way to my living room. Maybe it's hormones or just my incredible attraction to him, but part of me wishes he'd push me against the wall and take what he wants again. "I guess you're here to do some actual talking. No running?"

He sits on the couch and spreads his arms on the top like he owns the place. "No more running from this. Let's chat."

I sit in the tiny wingback chair across from him. Once I'm in the seat, I realize how much more comfortable the couch is. I eye his arms over the back of the couch and wish I could curl up next to him and feel those arms wrap around me while I bury my face in his chest and cry every worry and fear away.

"I'm sorry," I say, practically a whisper.

He squints. "For what?"

"For getting pregnant."

"I assume you aren't on birth control."

I chuckle and look out my nearby window, cringing as I notice I need to clean the glass. "I *assumed* I couldn't get pregnant after the endometriosis hell I went through in my late teens, and a doctor *assumed* that I would have fertility issues. You *assumed* I was on birth control. I guess it's true what they say about assuming – it makes an ass out of you and me. We all assumed and are definitely asses now."

"I didn't mean to make it sound like I was blaming you. It's my fault as much as it is yours. I could have pulled out. I could have used a condom. This is on both of us. I didn't mean it to sound so sexist."

He drums his fingers on the couch upholstery as we sit in silence for a few moments. Cars honk going by outside, and a bird chirps just outside the window. We both hold our breath, probably waiting for the other to speak.

"What do you want to do?" he finally whispers. "You sounded like you weren't sure you want to have it when we were at the doctor's office."

I look at the floor. "I don't know. I was kind of hoping you'd give me guidance because I honestly can't decide. I go back and forth."

"That's a lot of pressure on me."

"Suck it up because I've had a lot of pressure on me the last few weeks with trying to figure out how to tell you and what to do."

"Fair enough. Did you make a pros and cons list?"

I smirk. "How do you know me so well already?"

"You seem the type, and it's my job to know people. What were the pros?"

I hold up my hand and tick the items off as I look at the ceiling and try to remember what I wrote down in a journal entry I discarded last week. "I may never get pregnant again, so this is probably my only chance to have a child. I mean, I really think it was a fluke and all the stars aligned given my history."

"Valid," he nods.

I hold up another finger. "Lorelei says medical care could have changed in the last thirty years, so my birth experience may not be as scary as my mother's." I pause and look around the room. "That's it. I had two items on the pro list."

"The cons?" he asks.

"I had an entire page of those. I can't afford it. I could run into the same health issues as my mother. I'm not exactly known for great responsibility, so I'm not sure what kind of mother I'll make." I take a breath. "Those were just the top items."

"Why didn't you tell me?"

I inhale and finally look at him, expecting angry eyes. But his face is kind. Hurt. Damn, I didn't want to hurt him. "I was scared. I wanted it all to go away so we could just date since it was going so well."

"We can still date, Kailee. Nothing has to change about that."

My hands grip the cushion under me. "No, we can't."

"What do you mean we can't? Are we not having this baby?"

"Whether we have the baby or not is irrelevant. Dating is complicated now."

"What the fuck?" Chase mumbles under his breath, shaking his head.

"We can't date because I'll never again know if you're just dating me out of obligation because of the baby. I don't want to start a relationship like that."

He brings his arms down from the back of the sofa and cracks each knuckle in turn. "Do you think I don't want to get to know you now? Don't want to date you? Jesus fucking Christ, Kailee,

I told you the morning before I found out that I wanted to be with you."

"Yeah!" I yell. I pull at the hem of my shirt in frustration. "Just us. Not a baby in between us. It was all fine as long as it was a typical dating scenario. It's not. You may hate me in six months, but you'll feel like you have to stay now. I don't want to be your obligation, Chase. I've seen it a million times with friends and extended family. They get married because someone got pregnant, and they end up hating each other. One or both cheat and they end up divorced and fighting a shitty custody battle that leaves everyone bloody and scarred, even the kid. I don't want that."

"What do you want then?" he asks, raising his voice and scooting to the edge of his seat. "Tell me what to do, and I'll do it."

"Do you want this child?" I ask. I hold my breath, and my vision tunnels so he's the only thing I can see. There is no room around us. There's only Chase in front of me.

"Yes," he says in a suddenly quiet voice. "I've had a few days to think, and I want it. I'm willing to take custody and are willing to go through birth."

"What?" I yell. "If I'm risking my life and health to have this baby, I'm damn well going to raise it!" I yell. "How dare you?"

Chase runs his hands through his hair and stands. He paces in front of the couch much like he did at the doctor's office. Great. I reproduced with a pacer.

"I'm not trying to be an asshole. No matter what I say, it comes out wrong. I'm just saying that I'll be happy to do whatever you want. What do you mean when you say health issues?"

"It doesn't matter."

"It does to me!" he yells. "You matter to me."

"Only because I'm pregnant."

Chase pinches the bridge of his nose and makes a humming sound. "Is this some kind of hormonal thing? This irrational back and forth?"

"Irrational? Hormonal? Do you even hear yourself?"

He rolls his neck and rubs his shoulders, humming again. That must be an *angry Chase* thing. "Yes, I fucking hear myself. I just told you I want the baby! I asked you what your opinion is. What do you want? Tell me what it is. I'll do it. I'll do it, and I'll never make a peep if it's something I don't want. You're the one having to carry and give birth."

"If you want it, I'll have it."

"Fine." He throws up his hands. "Let's have a baby!"

"Fine!" I yell.

"When are you moving in?"

I lurch back like he punched me. "What?"

"When are you moving in?" he asks again. He crosses his arms over his chest.

"Why in the ever-loving fuck would I move in with you?"

He shrugs. "Why wouldn't you? It'll be easier to care for the baby, and we can get to know each other better. It'll be hard getting up and down these stairs when you're further along, and I want to keep you safe. It's a win-win."

"It's a lose-lose. We'll just end up resenting each other."

"How do you know that? We got along great before I knew you were pregnant. It'll be easier if I can get up with the baby at night with you or change a diaper or...something. I don't know what babies do."

I shake my head and chew on the inside of my cheek. "I don't want you to feel obligated to me because of this baby."

"I don't feel obligated. You're being ridiculous! I want to be a part of this."

I glare at him and tap my own foot before crossing my arms over my chest, mirroring his pose. "If I wasn't pregnant, would you have just asked me to move in with you?"

His mouth opens and then closes. The expression is so fish-like that I stifle a chuckle in my fist. He blinks a few times until I clear my throat. "That's what I thought. I don't want me being pregnant to dictate our relationship." Sudden sadness seeps into my heart because I realize that Chase and I will always just be about the baby now. Not about getting to know each other outside of it. There will never be the *just us* he asked for the morning before he found out.

We glare at each other a few moments before I walk to the door. I open it and wave in the direction of the hallway. "I guess we're having a baby, but I will not move in with you. I will not do anything with you that I feel like you wouldn't ask if we weren't having a child together. I can't. I can't put myself in that position. I want love, Chase. Not obligation. Everyone deserves to be loved."

He huffs and shakes his head in silence as he stomps toward the door. When he's a foot away, he flexes his fingers like he wants to touch me. I understand that feeling because I want to touch him, but does he only want to touch me now because I'm carrying his child? I don't want that. I want *him*. I want him to love me for me, not my stretching uterus.

"See you at work tomorrow," I say, looking at his chest. I won't look into his eyes.

He sighs and reaches toward me. I think he'll touch my cheek or push a lock of my hair back from my face, but he lowers his hand at the last second and shoves it into his pocket. "Yeah. See you at work."

Chapter 19

CHASE

I'm set to catch another crop of fornicating juveniles when Jeff Richter's arm is suddenly in front of my face as he leans against the wall, blocking passage to the staff bathrooms. "Mr. Barnett, we'd love it if you could join a small staff meeting in the lounge. We need to discuss, uh, the new vape cartridges we've seen in the news."

"OK." I draw out the word, looking left to right. This is weird.

I glance at the restrooms and lament I can't get in there and crack down before a teen pregnancy happens, but if the boss needs me in the lounge, I should go to the lounge. It's my last day here, and if there's one thing teens are good at, it's sneaking around and having sex with or without an adult busting them in the act. It's a tale as old as time and won't stop any time soon.

I trudge behind him as he talks about which teachers he thinks will retire at the end of this year and the new math curriculum not being approved by the board, even after hours of review and consultation on it. By the time I'm in front of the lounge door, I'm so bored that I could punch Jeff Richter. The only good thing I can say about him is that at least he doesn't talk shit about Kailee. He seems to have given up. I haven't heard him talk about her, and I haven't seen him lurking around her room or craning his head for a glimpse of her when she's nearby.

Only Leo does that now.

Jeff flings the door open, and I step into the room, expecting to find a couple resource officers from neighboring schools and a few members of the counseling staff. What I find is every staff member who has a plan period this hour or can duck out for a few minutes.

"Surprise!" They all shriek and then look around the room like they realize they're using their outside voices.

One of the gym teachers rolls over a cart with a cake on it. It's a sheet cake with white icing and something I can't read in blue letters. A decorative police car is in the corner of the cake. It's sweet, even if it resembles a toddler's birthday cake.

I quickly look around the room, searching for the one person I want to see. I'm always searching for her. I find Leo Paulson leaning against the wall, a smile on his face as he gives a wry wave he'd probably like to make with one finger. I shake my head and look past him until a teacher moves, and I finally see a wan Kailee seated at the table.

She smiles at me, but it's not a real smile. It doesn't reach her eyes. She's pale, and her lips almost match the color of her skin. Is she sick again? Is the nausea medicine the doctor gave her not working? Is she still angry with me after our argument last night? Did she sleep?

Fuck knows I didn't sleep last night. I tossed and turned, desperately wanting her next to me. I want her in my arms. I want to feel her body next to mine and hear her whisper to me in the middle of the night that she wants me. Our eyes lock for a moment, and I open my mouth to speak and tell her I'm sorry.

Our coworkers crowd around me with smiles and best wishes. They thank me for temping with pats on my back, handshakes, and questions about my excitement to go back to work with drug dealers and traffickers. I joke that drug dealers and traffickers don't buy me cake, and everyone laughs.

Everyone but her.

Well, Leo doesn't laugh, but who gives a shit about him?

One of the choir teachers shushes everyone and starts singing some kind of goodbye song. I've never been great about hearing "Happy Birthday." Somehow, this is more awkward because I don't know the words. I nod and smile as best I can.

Kailee gets up from her chair like she'll greet me. Is she coming to talk to me? Hug me goodbye and treat me like just another coworker and not the guy who impregnated her on my kitchen counter?

Whatever the reason, she stands in the middle of the song, and I cock my head and smile, wanting her to feel welcome to talk to me, even if it's to tell me to fuck off.

I see the look on her face I've seen more than a few times in my life. My mother faints a lot. She hits the linoleum every time she stands up too fast. I recognize the blank expression immediately – like someone's there but not there. I watch the color drain from Kailee's face like water being poured from a bucket. Her eyes go blank, practically rolling back in her head, and her knees buckle as I reach for her.

I'm too late. She falls to the old tile floor in a heap. I hover over her a second later as I ignore the shrieks and mumblings of, "Oh my God. Do we call an ambulance?" I roll her and slap her cheek lightly as I press my ear to her chest, my own heart pounding so hard in my ears that I wouldn't know if there was a problem with hers. Frantic, I press my fingers to her neck and find a strong pulse. She breathes in steady breaths, her chest rising and falling normally.

I close my eyes for a second and revel in the feel of her heart-beat that's strong and steady. She just passed out.

"Out of the way!" Leo yells behind me. "I know CPR."

He kicks me out of the way, and I stumble to the side. I roll out of my squat and put my hand out to catch myself, nailing him with a glare as the small circle that's formed around Kailee backs away. I can't blame them since they just saw their shop teacher kick their resource officer out of the way. A couple math teachers cover their mouths in shock.

Leo crouches over Kailee's body and positions her head so it's straight and up. "Kailee, baby, I'm going to do CPR!" he yells like she's either dead or has lost her hearing.

"The fuck you will," I say, grabbing his shirt at the shoulder. "She just passed out. She's breathing normally with a strong pulse. I know CPR. I've saved my partner's life with it, and everyone trained in it knows you only do CPR if they aren't breathing. Leave her be until she can be checked out by a medical staff."

"I'm going to save her!" he yells again, this time sticking his finger in the air like he has a brilliant idea.

I lean closer to his face and grip his shirt harder. If he leans down to put his mouth on her, he'll eat his fucking teeth.

"You don't need to save her, you dumb mother fucker. Leave her alone!" I yell back, my spit hitting his cheek.

"You're just jealous because you don't want my mouth on her!"

"You're right! I also don't want you to break her fucking ribs during chest compressions."

"I won't hurt her!"

"You do know that CPR sometimes has that unintended consequence, right? You only use it when you have to, and she doesn't need it!"

"I'm her friend!" he yells.

"I'm a first responder and have had way more training than you!" I look around at the crowd. They seem to be on my side as they nod when I mention more training. I look at a woman I know as a history teacher. "Go get Becky in the nurse's office."

The woman nods and hustles out the back door of the lounge that connects the lounge to a long hallway and leads to the nurse's area.

"She needs CPR!" Leo desperately pleads.

"Don't you fucking touch her," I say, dropping my voice and getting close to his face so that our noses almost touch. "You could hurt her, and she doesn't need it."

Leo grips my wrist and tries to pull my hand off his shirt, but I hang on. "Who the fuck are you?" he asks. "You don't even work here full-time."

I grit my teeth. "She's pregnant, and I'm the father. That's who the fuck I am. Get your hands off her before I make this embarrassing."

Somewhere behind me, I hear Jeff's voice mumble to another teacher, "I thought he said she was a lesbian."

"Was she inseminated with his sperm?" another unknown teacher asks. I don't look to who says it because I'm still staring down Leo.

Something changes in Leo Paulson's face. His eyes go wide, and he turns the same color as Kailee did before she went down. Then, even as I watch, his face turns a beet red that screams extreme embarrassment or irrational anger. Judging by the way his hand tightens around my wrist and his teeth bare so I can see his early gum disease, it's the latter.

"You mother fucker," he whispers. "We never even had a chance with her, did we?"

"Why did you ever think you would?" I growl back, my own lip curled.

He pushes me away from him, but I hold on to his shirt enough to hear the light ripping sound of the fabric as I fall back, bringing him with me.

Fine. We may be sprawled on the teacher's lounge floor in a sexually suggestive position as my legs frantically try to move away from him, but at least he's on top of me instead of Kailee.

People gasp and sputter as they freeze, unsure of what to do when it's their coworkers involved in such shenanigans.

Something is wrong with Leo, though. His eyes are wild, and he tries to pin my arms down before realizing it's fruitless. I'm too strong for him.

Nearby, Jeff and a male science teacher inch closer, probably hoping they don't have to pull us apart. One of the counselors leans down to help Leo stand, but Leo slaps the man's hand away. He looks around the room, practically panting, and finally averts his eyes to Kailee's still form. "I'll still save her!" he roars before moving off of me in an impressive roll a military officer would envy.

He hovers over Kailee's still form and is about six inches away from putting his mouth on hers when I've had enough. Standing up, I grab him by the scruff of his shirt until he's also in standing position, and I spin him to face me. His hands move wildly through the air like defective windmills. I push them away without consideration for his fucking feelings before deciding that I have to keep him away from Kailee. She could get hurt, and she comes first.

Kailee and my child.

I pull my arm back to get momentum and then punch Leo Paulson straight in the nose.

He goes down, and I spread my legs, standing over him as he shakes his head and checks his face. Blood runs out of his nose, and every person in the room except Jeff Richter backs against the wall in a circle reminiscent of kindergarten story time or a crowded game of *Duck Duck Goose.*

"Don't you touch her again," I warn, pointing at him.

He slowly struggles to right himself, as I move into a stance I'm trained for. Suspects take swings at me all the time. We go through hours of training, and I'm ready for him as he quickly gets to his feet, brushes off his pants like he's not going to do anything, and then fakes out going one direction before tackling me around my waist.

I know how to handle the move since I was expecting it. It's a simple twisting motion and hitting his pressure points to release me before using his momentum against him.

I just forgot about the damn cake cart behind us.

We both crash into the cart and gasps of horror fill my ears. One teacher starts to cry, and I wonder if she's crying over the fight or if she's crying because there will definitely be no cake eating today as the cake topples to the floor in what seems like slow motion. Something cool and mushy covers my face and oozes down the back of my neck. I flail, trying to find purchase and get off the floor, but Leo holds me down and the icing isn't helping either of us move.

I roll, making a bigger mess, and I frantically try getting into a pushup position to get out of this shit. It's hard to do since I'm not sure exactly how unhinged he is, and I'm armed with both a gun and a taser. I frantically protect both weapons by keeping my arms at my sides. My left hand grapples for the taser, but my fingers are so slick that I can't grip it enough to get it out of the holster.

"I'll kill you, you dickhead!" Leo yells close to my ear.

Out of the corner of my eye, I notice staff members holding up their phones. Great. Richter's feet shuffle nearby, and I realize he's trying to pull us apart without covering himself with cake. He claps his hands and says something I can't hear since I have devil's food cake in my ears. Another teacher tries to help but quickly falls on his ass in the cake mess on the floor, dropping a cuss word as he falls.

Leo, however, is crazed. He pushes my face into what's left of the cake and screams, "Die, womanizer! How dare you defile her like that?"

I only see cake in front of me until I squeeze my eyes shut. It fills my nose and mouth as Leo's hand holds my head down. I can't breathe. This is how I'm going to die. I've been shot, stabbed, and severely beaten by drug dealers and gang members in my day, but I'm going to be suffocated to death by cake at the hands of an angry shop teacher.

Like fucking hell.

I finally turn my face enough to my side where I can gasp for breath and not die by cake drowning, but cake is all over my face, in my hair, and a quick look at the front of my shirt shows I'm coated in it. I spit, and a chunk drops from my mouth.

Still, Leo hangs on.

"Jesus Christ, were you a wrestler in high school?" I sputter, finally able to speak.

Pain shoots through my back shoulder and I realize Leo has his teeth in me. "Are you fucking biting me, you nutcase?"

I roar as he sinks his teeth further into my shoulder like a deranged *Twilight* fan on bath salts. I shimmy my shoulder and elbow Leo in the chest repeatedly, but he's like my drugged-up criminals – entirely out of control and running on adrenaline.

I roar in anger and try shaking him off again, but it hurts worse to move with his canines in my shoulder.

Thankfully, he's just as covered in cake, and his grip around the nape of my neck loosens as I wiggle. His teeth eventually leave my skin as I elbow him again. I kick out at him, kneeing him in the balls so that I can get up. He groans and drops his hands to cover his dick.

My knees slide in the buttercream icing, but I'm eventually able to get to my feet, slipping and sliding so much I hold onto a nearby table.

Unfortunately, Leo also gets up, nostrils flaring and face red like a charging bull. He gets into a crouch position and comes at me again to grab my waist, but there's no cake behind me this time. This time, I grab his shoulders and spin him so his momentum works against him. He falls into a nearby candy bar machine, leaving a trail of icing on the floor. Several candy bars rattle out of their slots and fall into the dispenser as the entire machine wobbles.

It happens in slow motion, and Leo gets out of the way a split second before it falls halfway to the ground with half getting caught on a nearby table. The glass shatters, and candy bars spill onto the floor, mixing with the icing.

Leo ignores his brush with death. He gets up again, and I ready a punch, only to find Jeff's face in front of me as soon as I throw it. I can't stop the momentum, and Jeff is too slow to block it.

"Shit!" I yell as Jeff also goes down, blood splattering on the floor and mixing with white icing.

I cover my mouth with my hands and cuss again under my breath as one of the administrative assistants helps him up.

"Do we call the police?" someone asks, their voice frantic.

"He is the police," another person answers. "I think we're kind of fucked."

Leo doesn't care about any talk about police, doesn't care I'm an officer, and obviously doesn't give one shit about Jeff Richter's broken nose, the cake on the floor, or the broken vending machine. He's like a formerly caged animal that's just been let loose after years of abuse.

He barrels at me again and takes a kick at my balls that's almost laughable. I'm able to bat his leg away, and his shoes squeak against the floor as he falls, this time landing on his back. He wobbles up, and I have just enough time to grip my taser and aim it at him.

The coils release from the taser and the tell-tale sound of someone being electrocuted fills the room. Women scream. Jeff Richter screams like a woman. Eyes are wide around me, and mouths are covered in shock as Leo Paulson shakes and then hits the ground, a hunk of drool dropping down from his mouth.

I stare at him a moment to make sure he's alive, and he blinks up at me. "Stay down, douchebag," I growl through gritted teeth.

I give a cursory nod to Jeff as he stands but otherwise ignore every other person in the room as I move to Kailee again.

"Kailee, can you hear me?" I ask, lightly slapping her cheek again. Her eyes flutter open and then immediately close again like she can't keep them open.

I look around the room and at my coworkers who are still in some state of shock. Some glance at the cake all over the floor. Others stare at Kailee. The pot-smoking art teacher crouches over the broken vending machine and stuffs candy bars into his button-down shirt.

Several people are still taking video.

"Where's the nurse?" I ask.

"She had some pukers about an hour ago. Maybe she's busy with that?" someone answers. "She wasn't in her office. Could be at lunch."

I inhale and then blow out the long breath. "Kailee, I'm going to pick you up and take you to the hospital. I got you."

She's still out for the count, so I carefully lift her in my arms like she's nothing. Her long lashes flutter against her cheeks, and she curls into me like she feels safe against my body.

Someone opens the lounge door for me and I walk into the hallway...during passing period.

"What the fuck?" a kid I know as a sophomore asks before jumping out of the way.

Cake drips from my face and onto Kailee as I carefully walk through the halls. I can feel icing in my ear and inside my nose. A mixture of both cake and icing is stuck to my own lashes, and I frantically blink it away.

Shouts of my name and questions about what happened follow us down the hallway. Some of the teen girls say Kailee's name, obviously concerned at why a cake-covered man is carrying her still form down the hall. Every student backs away from us and looks at the floor as I leave a trail of mess behind us.

"Everything's fine. Just fine." The front door is fifty feet away. Just a bit further. "Go to class. This is just an unfortunate accident. Everything is fine," I say as I walk as fast as I can with icing coating the soles of my shoes.

I eventually get out of the building and quickly hustle to the cruiser. Thankfully, I have a special parking spot as the resource officer. Students flock to the side windows and watch as I round the car to the passenger side and gently place Kailee in the front seat before circling the car and opening the driver's door.

I wave at the students and put on my best smile the drying icing will allow me to give. "See you later. It's all good."

A few kids wave back, and I give a thumbs-up signal before ducking into my car.

"This is one mother fucker of a day, huh, sweetheart?" I say to a silent Kailee as I buckle her seat belt, start my car, and turn on my siren. She shifts in her seat and mumbles something before putting her face against the passenger side window. As soon as I pull away from the school, I press the button for my car's hand-free phone function and call Liam.

Chapter 20

KAILEE

I blink at the bright lights above me, only to find Liam's face so close to me that I yelp and push back against something soft behind my head. Pillows? Behind him, Lorelei stares at me, her mouth slightly open. Memories of whispering from moments before bop around my head. They were talking about me and why I'm here. They were talking about Chase.

"Where am I, and why are you so close to my face?"

"You're in the hospital," Lorelei says, moving into better view. Liam moves aside and lets Lorelei sit on the edge of my bed. "You weren't feeling well at work and passed out. They think it was low blood pressure and low blood sugar."

That makes sense. I've been woozy when standing too fast for a few days, and I haven't been keeping much down when I can bear to eat. My pregnancy book says low blood pressure is common in early pregnancy, and the nurse at the doctor's office mentioned mine was a bit low when I was there. One more thing to be mindful of. My thoughts swirl in my mind. Low blood pressure now and the worry of high blood pressure later. Fuck, this pregnancy stuff is hard on a woman's body.

"How did I get here?" I ask.

Please don't let them tell me it was an ambulance. I can't imagine the medical bill. My toes curl under the blanket as I brace myself for the amount of money I'll owe for a cross-town jaunt to the hospital for something that routinely happens to pregnant women.

"Chase picked you up and brought you. Carried you through the doors and everything." God, Lorelei and the Chase hero worship again. I guess he's off her shit list. "He stayed until we got here, and they kicked him out about twenty minutes ago and made him go wash the cake out of his hair. He was causing quite the mess. Incidentally, your favorite sweater now smells like buttercream," Lorelei says.

My nose crinkles. "Do I want to know why he was covered in cake and why I have to throw away my sweater?"

Lorelei puts her hands on her hips and grimaces. "No, you do not."

"How long was I out?"

"About an hour. Chase got you in the car and put his police light on. They said you passed out and then were probably so tired you stayed out even when you could have come to." I look around the room. I'm not hooked to anything electrical, but I have an IV dripping something into the vein of my left hand. "Oh, you were dehydrated, too. They're giving you fluids."

I don't doubt that as much as I throw up.

"Is the baby OK?" I squeak.

Lorelei nods. "Right as rain. You need a little work, though. You had a blood pressure blip and are so severely dehydrated that they were kind of impressed you went to work and were functional for half a day. The baby is OK, though. Your heart rate is good."

I nod and look around the standard hospital room. A small chair is nearby, and the Missouri River is outside my window, showcasing a beautiful fall day. The smell of cleaner fills my nose, and I cough. That's not going to help the nausea.

"Can I go home now that I'm awake?"

"The doctor said he'd be back to check on you. They said they'd release you after the fluids," Lorelei says.

"Since we have time to kill, tell me what happened with Chase."

Lorelei sits in the extra chair and holds her hands out like she's going to tell a grand story. "Apparently, Chase Barnett defended your honor."

"I wouldn't go that far," Liam mumbles as he moves to her side and props himself on the arm of the chair. "He took a swipe at that guy at work, though."

"Leo? He hit Leo?"

"Got a decent knock to the principal in, too," he chuckles. He quickly straightens his face when he sees I find nothing funny about any of this. "The principal was trying to pull them apart."

"Why were they fighting?"

"Well, when you passed out, Leo wanted to give you CPR," Lorelei explains. "Chase didn't want your ribs broken."

"Excuse me? I passed out. I wasn't having a heart attack."

"That's what Chase said. He checked for a pulse, and yours was steady. You were breathing. There was really nothing to do but get you to the hospital to have you checked. He explained that to Leo, but Leo still wanted to put his mouth on yours."

I make a gagging gesture at the idea of Leo explaining to our coworkers why he should put his mouth on mine. "Ew. Please tell me he didn't stick his tongue down my throat. I feel violated."

Lorelei shakes her head so hard that her ponytail hits her cheeks. "No way. Chase wouldn't let it happen. There was some pushing and shoving." Lorelei's face is pink, and she practically pants with excitement to tell the story of how Chase protected me from Leo Paulson's midday coffee breath. "Well, Chase wouldn't have him touch you like that, so he punched him."

"Right there in the teacher's lounge?"

She nods, her eyes wide. Liam shakes his head like he can't believe it.

"Leo didn't like that," Lorelei continues. She puts her hands out in front like a tribal elder of centuries ago telling stories about wolves and the grandfathers around a fire before a big hunt. "He attacked Chase, ripping and kicking." She pantomimes punching and kicking. "Chase had teeth marks on his shoulder, so there was obvious biting. Leo was an enraged animal!"

I put my hand over my chest and grimace. "What the hell? Are you fucking with me right now? In front of everyone?"

Liam shakes his head. "Not fucking with you."

"Leo pushed Chase into the cake cart and then jumped on him," Lorelei continues. "They thrashed around like...like a stallion going at a mare in heat."

Liam side eyes his girlfriend with a questioning look. Lorelei notices, shakes her head, and glares at him. "Do you have a better analogy, Liam?"

"Do horses go into heat?" he asks.

She shakes her head and shrugs. "I don't really know. Google it." She turns her attention back to me. "But they went after it, rolling around in the cake as their hands and bodies were slathered in buttercream, Chase defending you from that awful predator."

"This is awfully descriptive for a woman who wasn't even there and is going off a thirty-second run down from Chase," Liam says.

"Shut up, Liam. This story is legendary now. You can't stop that. Your partner is a hero. First, he saved your life, and now he defends Kailee when she's incapacitated. He should be the new Captain America, and you'll never convince me otherwise."

"So, Leo rolled Chase around in the cake, and Chase eventually picked me up and put me in his police cruiser?"

"Yep," Lorelei says, nodding. "Well, after he tased Leo."

"He tased Leo?" Dear Christ, this will be the fodder for teacher's lounge conversation for a long time.

"He drove you straight here, called us, and called ahead to have orderlies waiting. They used smelling salts and everything. Who knew those still existed?"

"I came to? Why don't I remember?"

Lorelei shrugs. "You focused your eyes and then went right back to sleep. Have you been sleeping at all?"

"Very little."

Lorelei gets out of her chair and approaches my bed. She smoothes the sheet a bit before sitting down. "You have to start taking this seriously and taking care of your body. I know the nausea thing is bad, but you need sleep. Water when you throw up. Chase said you're keeping the baby."

"Yeah, we're keeping it."

Liam clears his throat. "He also said you fought because you don't think you should be a couple."

I stare at my hand and the needle sticking out of it. "It sounds bad when you say it like that."

"Because it is bad," Lorelei says.

Liam stretches his long legs out and slouches into the chair Lorelei vacated. He puts his hands behind his head like he's on vacation. "Do you want to know what he says about you?"

I raise my head, suddenly interested.

Liam doesn't wait for me to answer. "Mind you, this is before he found out you were pregnant. This information is from seeing him in passing over the last couple of weeks when we've had to go to our separate counseling sessions. It's from my party Lorelei threw."

Lorelei scoots to the edge of the bed and fidgets with her dress. Our eyes never leave Liam, and Lorelei holds her breath, waiting for the information about what Chase feels. My heart pounds with the fact that Chase Barnett has talked about me.

Liam smiles at both Lorelei and me and takes a deep breath. "He said he thought he finally found someone who makes him happy. He said you were a challenge and stubborn as a mule, but he's never been so captivated. Like he had to get to know you and had to learn whatever he could about you. He said you wouldn't tell him things about yourself, and he asked me. He asked me if you have family nearby. He asked if I knew how you got started substitute teaching. He asked me if you wanted kids before he even knew you were knocked up."

He stops for a second and looks me straight in the eyes. "If he's not one-hundred-percent head over heels in love with you yet, he will be soon if you even give him one iota of a chance to prove himself. And he will prove himself. He's not a villain.

He's not evil. He wants you – has wanted you for a while. His eyes light up when he sees you. I have known him for a few years now. I've been through everything with the guy. We've picked up women together when we were both single, been on drug busts, sat through stakeouts, and worked through some intense undercover gigs. I've never seen his eyes follow someone through a room like he does when you walk in. I saw it when you and Lorelei came back from the kitchen at my party."

I work the hospital blanket between my fingers. "He said all of this before he found out?"

Liam nods. "He's not faking it, and I don't know if you'll ever get rid of him, Kailee. Whatever you think about him *only* liking you because of the baby, it's bullshit."

Lorelei nods nearby. "You have to get out of your head about it, Kailee. Let him love you for you. Let him take care of you."

"You're one to talk. Talk about independent and stubborn!"

"Don't I know it," Liam says under his breath, earning a middle finger from Lorelei.

"I may be independent and stubborn, but if a couple of people I trusted said something, I'd believe them," Lorelei says. "If you can't trust him yet, trust us that he's a good guy and obviously cares for you, baby or no baby."

"He'll be a good father," Liam says. "But he's also a good partner. I should know. He's my work partner. He's wanted someone for a relationship for a long time, and I think he met you and just...fell hard."

My stomach turns, and it doesn't have anything to do with morning sickness.

What have I done? I've been so busy trying to create the perfect relationship timeline that I rejected a great guy and the father of my child because he wanted to help me.

I've never been helped before. What's help? Is this what it's like to be loved? Knowing that I have a rough life and it will be infinitely less rough if I form a team with the one person who is attractive, dead sexy, and just wants me in his orbit?

This isn't about my child. This is about my stupidity – my inability to believe someone wants me just because I've never felt wanted before.

Chase Barnett wants me.

Me!

He wants me for who I am and not who some dickhead wants me to be. He doesn't want my boobs to be bigger or my teeth to be perfectly white. He doesn't want me to have a better job or a better education. He doesn't care that I'm broke.

He wants to care about...me.

Love me?

I look back at Liam and inhale deeply. "I trust you, so don't bullshit me. If I miscarried right this second, would Chase still date me and even still ask me to move in with him? Maybe not right this second, but eventually? Even after all I've put the guy through the last week?"

Liam leans forward in his chair and rests his elbows on his knees. He looks into my eyes and doesn't blink. "Yes."

"How are we doing in here?" a voice chimes from the doorway. A handsome doctor sashays into the room, but I don't flirt like I normally would. There's only one man I want to flirt with.

"How long until I can get out of here?" I ask.

The doctor thumps the IV and pulls up my chart on his iPad. "We need the whole IV to run. After that, you can leave, but I want you to go straight home and rest until we get the blood work results back."

"How long do I have to rest?"

"Twenty-four hours."

Good. That gives me enough time to craft a decent apology to the best man I've ever met.

Chapter 21

KAILEE

"This is me eating shit," I say as soon as Chase opens the door.

He blinks twice like he's not sure if I'm real and then looks left and right up the street. I shuffle the bouquet of gourmet popcorn out from under my armpit and hold it out to him. "Lorelei told me what you did. How you carried me into the hospital."

He takes the popcorn and steps back, a silent gesture that I can come into his house.

His living room is dim, and food containers litter every surface.

"Are you OK?" I ask.

He snorts a sarcastic laugh. "No, I am not, in any capacity, OK." He slinks onto the sofa, setting the popcorn on a small spot on the end table where it barely fits. "It's safe to say I won't ever be a resource officer again."

"Did you get fired from the force?" I ask in a whisper.

"No. I'm too good of a drug agent for that. My boss wasn't pleased though. He said I made him look stupid in front of his golf buddy, the superintendent of schools."

"Ah. Great. The superintendent knows who I am."

Chase sighs and runs his hand through his hair. "Relax. Nobody could possibly blame you for me clocking Leo and causing the destruction of the teacher's lounge."

"You could blame me. I took him up on that date so I could make you mad."

Chase furrows his brow. "You went out with him to make me jealous? I thought you were just pissed because I told you about the bet those guys had?"

I wave my hands in the air like I'm being attacked by a sudden swarm of bees. "You know what? It doesn't matter.

"He got fired, by the way."

"Really?" I ask. Even though he went absolutely crazy at the end, I still feel bad for Leo.

He nods and chuckles. "My boss isn't super happy about the videos that are circulating, but the staff all said I was doing the right thing and just defending you. At the end of the day, that's my job, and I did it. People have it on video and saw him threaten to do CPR on you when you didn't need it and also got him trying to drown an officer with cake. I think the biting me like a rabid dog was the nail in the coffin. You should also know I'm now a viral YouTube star."

"You're kidding."

"You're looking at Hot Cake Cop."

"Well, there goes your undercover career."

"Why are you here, Kailee? I think you made it clear you don't want much from me no matter how hard I try. I promise not to leave you to parent by yourself, but you really did a number on me, you know? I just wanted to be with you."

Fuck, his words are like a punch to the face. I take a deep breath. "It's time I stop running from the decision, and it's time I start speaking to you like you're a partner in this. I've acted like a child, and I've treated you like shit, which is crazy because I absolutely adore you, Chase. I have since I saw you. I let my fear control my choices, and I didn't listen to my heart, my friends who I really trust, or the one person I should have been listening to." I wave my hand up and down his body. "That's you, in case you were wondering."

I take another breath and straighten my shoulders. "I think you'll be a good dad. I'm scared and unsure I can support a child, and we obviously have issues between us -

He holds up a hand, interrupting me. "I don't think that. The issues, I mean. I think we get along like a house on fire when you're not assuming I'm just in this for the baby, and I think we'd be great together. Parents or not, I think we just fit." He looks at his feet like the answer to our big question is written on the top of his shoes.

"It'll be hard enough to finish out this pregnancy with what I know about my family history, but I will. I may need extra medical care, and I'd like to talk about possible help if I have to have a c-section or have outrageous hospital bills. I don't know what will happen to our relationship, but I'm over here just trying to figure out how to navigate having a son."

Chase's head pops up. "Son?"

"Yeah, they did a bunch of tests on me to test if I had any nutritional deficiencies. It's a boy. At least, there's a seventy percent chance it's a boy at this point in the pregnancy. It'll be more certain in a few weeks." I squint. "Do not tell me that makes a difference. If you're telling me you care it's a boy and not a girl..."

He holds his hands up, and I stop midsentence. He shakes his head. "I don't care. I'd like a girl just the same, but it...makes it more real for me."

I slink down in front of him onto his coffee table like my legs are buckling out from under me. "Yeah, me too. That's part of why I'm here and not at the abortion clinic across the river. I can't afford to be a good mother to him, Chase, but I wanted to give you the chance to be a good father, even if we end up heartbroken and hating each other. Part of me is scared of that happening, and that's why I was an asshole to you. But some women don't have a Chase in their life. Some women are left on their own and desperate. I'm lucky enough that I'm sitting across from you and having a discussion right now."

He scowls and clenches his jaw. "I want this baby, but I want you more. You know that, right? Even if you live separately from me while we figure this out, I want to try. But of fucking course I'll take care of you if you need postpartum care. Did I say that right? That's what it's called? Or did I just make up a new word?"

I nod and can't help but grin. "Have you been reading?"

He reaches under his couch cushion and pulls out a banged-up copy of *The Expectant Father*. He drops it on the coffee table and jerks his chin toward it. "Library sale."

"You're excited, aren't you?"

He meets my eyes, and I swear they sparkle. "I'm getting there. But here's the thing, Kailee – I'm more excited for *you*."

"What do you mean?"

He reaches under the couch again and brings out another beat-to-hell book. "They also had a copy of this book from the last century about winning the heart of the woman you love. It's a little outdated, but I –

I cut him off as I lean forward and press my lips to his. He meets my kiss, and I wrap my arms around his warm neck, hungrily taking everything he'll give me. He could touch me anywhere right now. Say anything. Our mouths mesh together, and I melt into him as he pulls me to his lap, his warm chest pressing against mine. I straddle him and run my hands over his face, down his jaw, up again, and through his hair.

When we finally pull apart, my face is wet with tears I didn't know I was shedding. He swipes his thumb through one. "What's this about?"

"I don't know what to believe. Do we jump full into trying to be together, or do we just worry about our son?"

He presses his forehead to mine and closes his eyes, humming a little as he smiles. "Why do you make everything so difficult and dramatic?"

Chapter 22

CHASE

Why the fuck is everything so black and white with her? No gray? Hard?

"I don't mean to be that way," she whimpers, and she wipes a tear off her face. "I think part of the problem is that I've wanted to be invisible my whole life. Tiptoe through, you know? Don't stay too long in a relationship enough to hurt someone or myself. Don't have kids. Don't get married. Don't even get a job where I'd have to stay and maybe make something of myself." She stutters a little as she says it, sobbing at the end.

"How's that working out for you?" I ask, wiping a lock of hair out of her face.

"It's shit," she sobs. Her lip trembles as she tries to speak. "But I don't know any other way, and everything in my fucked-up head told me to be afraid you only feel obligated to care about me."

I shake my head like a petulant child and flex my jaw. "That's bullshit, Kailee. I wanted you long before this baby came on the scene. Well, long before I knew there was a baby. I wanted a relationship with you when I saw you walking into that school one day. Did you know I used to watch you walk in from an upstairs window?" I ask. Another tear runs out of her eye, and I wipe it away with my thumb again. "You looked so beautiful. Kind. A smile for everyone. Like the woman I've always had it in my mind that I'd end up with. You're it. Baby or no baby, you're it. I knew when I took you to the hospital that I'd still love you, Kailee. I knew if you lost that baby, I'd still want you. I'd still bring you peanut butter and jelly sandwiches. I'd still tase Leo into next Tuesday to get a chance to be your hero. I want to try with you."

"How can you say that after all I've put you through?"

I jolt back a bit, my brow furrowed. "What, exactly, have you put me through?"

"Oh, I don't know," she says, waving her arms like a crazy person. My eyes flick to her stomach, worried too much stress will send her back to the hospital. "I ran out on you the night we met because I was stupid. I'm always so fucking stupid!" She holds up her hand and starts counting off items on her fingers. "I got pregnant. I listened to a dumb doctor who said I'd probably need fertility help to have a baby."

"You didn't make this baby by yourself. Personally, I blame your love of margaritas and my inviting kitchen counter."

"I made you scared for the baby."

"This has been insane for everyone. You've been shocked, scared, and in survival mode. I can empathize with that. I was terrified, Kailee. Hell, I still am, but I don't blame you for any of this."

She holds up her other hand. "I'm not done. I probably worried you sick at the hospital. I made you feel bad for telling me about that stupid bet with Leo. I –

I pull her to my chest, cutting her off. "I will always defend you. Whatever happens. I'm here, and I'm not going anywhere if you'll let me stay by your fucking side. When you have this baby, I'm going to be there in whatever capacity you want me. If you want me in the room and holding your hand, you got it. If you want me down the hall on a plastic chair drinking shit coffee until you're ready for me to see our baby, I'll stay up all night and pace holes in the floor. I'll be there.

"Then, when you come home, I'll get up with the baby. I'll clean the toilet. I'll make you food. If you have to have one of those cesarean things that are so hard on your body, I'll do all the chores, drive, and lift the baby for you. If you can't care for that baby because of any reason –depression, physical illness – I've got us."

"All birth is hard, Chase. A lot can go wrong with any way the baby comes out. It's part of why I hesitated. My mom had a rough time. She almost died, and I'm scared I'll be the same."

I give a short nod. "You're right. I'm sorry. It's not the first time I'll say those words to you. Your feelings are valid. I was wrong to assume you'd just move in because we're having a baby. You're your own person. I'm my own person. I shouldn't have tried to rush combining us into a family too fast."

She sighs and places her hands on my chest. "I need to know without circling it. No bullshit. Final answer. I need to hear it a final time. Do you just want me because of the baby?" she asks.

I look down at my shoes for a second and hope she doesn't think I'm being insincere. I just can't focus on her face when my eyes are so clouded with tears. I've cried more in the last few days than I have in my entire life. It's not because I'm scared of being a father. As she sits here on my lap, her arms around me, I realize it's because I'm scared of losing her.

I should answer her, but I need to tell her the truth. The full truth.

I raise my head and let her see my face. I let her see the look in my eyes so she knows I mean every word I'm going to say to her.

"I have wanted you for weeks. I knew I wanted you on our date when I kissed you and left you at the door. Our times enjoying each other after that, I wanted *you*. Think about how I looked at you. How I waved at you through your classroom window, wanting to fling the door open and kiss you in front of the students. In case you aren't keeping up, that was before I found out you're pregnant. Somewhere along the line, I decided that you're the person I want to try with, Kailee, and that timeline started long before I found out about the baby."

I pull her closer and don't blink. I'm so close that her eyes go wide, and I tilt her chin so she has to look at me. "Can't you accept that someone loves you for you? I enjoyed the hell out of fucking you the night we met, but you never left my mind. Was that lust? Sure was. But then I got to know you. I see you through Lorelei's eyes. I see you through your students' eyes. I wanted to tear Leo's and Jeff's balls off for even looking at you before I knew you were the mother of my child. I grew obsessed with you in a way I haven't been with another woman in my life. I love our child now, even if you don't yet. I think that's normal. If not, I know now it should be normalized. Not every child comes into this world riding a unicorn while people jump for joy, but I want it. More importantly, I want his mother more than anything in the universe."

She shakes so hard, trying to be strong. Her lip quivers again. I hand her a tissue and watch as she wipes her face with trembling hands.

It's my turn to ask.

"Do you care about *me*, or did you just want to get to know *me* because of the baby?" I ask. I need to know if I'm more invested than she is in this relationship. If it's one-sided, this won't work. "Did you only go out with me because you wanted to tell me but were too scared?"

She shakes her head and squeezes her eyes shut. "No, Chase. I wanted to be with you. In fact, I wished the baby would just go away so I could take it out of the equation and not have it be an issue. My heart shattered into a million pieces that morning when you said you wanted just us. I wanted to click my heels together and not have it be the thing you latched onto to stay with me."

"It's not. Period." I tilt her chin up so she has to look at me. "Do you at least see yourself falling for me?"

She sniffles so hard I worry she'll stop breathing. "Y-yes," she stammers. "Somewhere along the line, I fell in love with you, too."

"When was it?" I ask, shocking her into silence. She stops blubbering.

"What?"

"When was it you realized it wasn't just about the baby with me? I need to hear it, Kailee," I say, pressing my palm to my heart, partially to make sure it's still in my chest.

She idly touches a curl over my forehead, smoothing it back from my face. "When you showed up with that sandwich. Then, I started to watch my classroom door more than I paid attention to my students. I just wanted you to walk by. I wouldn't have told you about the baby at work in front of the students, so I knew it wasn't just about working up the balls to tell you. I wanted to see you walk by my classroom and smile at me. Maybe wave. It was the best part of my day when you did that."

I don't wait for permission or a fucking cue. I push off the couch and wrap my arms around her as I lift her. She wraps her legs around my waist as I walk through the kitchen and smile at the counter. "Want to for old time's sake?" I ask, jerking my chin in the direction of the blessedly clean counter.

"I think I prefer a bed this time."

I press my lips to hers and kiss her. When I pull my lips away, I trail them up her jaw. "As you wish."

I walk her to my bedroom and kick the door shut as I enter. I'm frantic for her but also hesitant. Will I hurt her? Will she hold back with me because we're now going to be someone's parents and parents don't have sex? I mean, everyone knows that. My parents don't. I'm certain of it.

I gently lay her on the bed and hover over her, boxing her in. I refuse to lie on top of her in case I hurt her, and I hold myself in plank position.

She giggles when she notices my shaking biceps. "You can come down, Chase."

"I don't want to hurt you."

"You won't. I'm not even showing."

"Yet," I whisper. I push myself to my knees and run my hands over her stomach, lifting her shirt. "I can't wait to see you pregnant, Kailee. I can't wait to touch you here, knowing it's my baby in there."

I slide down the bed, and she inhales, probably anticipating my mouth in all the right places. I'll get to that. I have a whole night with her. I have the next eight hours to show her just how much I'm falling for her and show her that I'm hers.

I place a soft kiss just under her belly button before kissing up until my head is practically under her shirt. She giggles and bends up, pulling her shirt over her head and throwing it across the room. I have her bra off in seconds, and I latch onto a nipple and palm the other breast as I suck, noticing her breasts are fuller than I remember them being since we were last in this room. I lap at her before I move up her neck and jaw.

She undoes my pants and pulls my cock from my boxer briefs, and I hiss against her ear. "Someone's awfully eager."

"Remember the workroom?" she asks. I nod against her face. "It gave me a new appreciation for pregnancy orgasms. I never shook like that before."

I push my pants all the way down my legs and hastily kick them somewhere into the void of my darkened room. She runs her hands up and down my back, through my hair, and down to my ass where she grabs handfuls of me, desperately pulling me to her.

I don't make her wait. I slide into her inch by inch and stroke her hair back from her face. "I'm here," I whisper, pushing my forehead to hers and swiveling inside of her. "I'm inside of you, I'm next to you when you hurt or are scared, and I'm behind you in every decision."

She gives a weak smile before her lip starts to tremble. I put my finger over it, silencing her before she cries. I only make women cry in bed when they come, and I'm not going to start making them cry with words now.

I press another kiss to her mouth, close my eyes, and rock into oblivion.

A Few Months Later

KAILEE

"**P**ush, Kailee. You got this," Chase says, wiping a drop of sweat off my face and pushing a strand of hair back that's stuck to my lip.

The hospital is short-staffed tonight. One nurse stands by, dedicated to caring for the baby. One nurse is helping the doctor and simultaneously supporting my other leg while the doctor is between my legs doing whatever doctors do down there.

My foot presses against Chase's chest, and he strokes my leg as he tells me to push. The stirrups weren't giving me enough leverage to bear down as much as I've needed to in the last hour. My legs needed to be higher. Fear settles into my chest, and I need this baby out. I'm scared I'll push this much and still need surgical intervention.

"Almost here, Kailee," Dr. Dewson says from down below. Not that I can really see her over my stomach.

I just want to put my head back and cry. I've spent a lot of the last hour with my eyes shut, willing this entire situation to just go away. This is already terrifying, and I almost lost it when they had to attach a heart monitor to the top of my baby's head while he's still inside of me. I don't know what I'd do if Chase hadn't held my hand all this time.

At least I'm not feeling any pain. I got the epidural and feel zero shame about it. It's allowed me to focus on how I'm feeling and enabled me to be present in the moment with Chase. Honestly, it's meant the world to me that I'm clear-headed and haven't been saddled with pain for the last twenty hours that I've been here since my water broke in our bed last night. I've had the chance to rest, even if I haven't slept, and Chase slept for a bit on the room's couch last night since I wasn't up hurting through contractions. I needed medicine to help me contract, and I've been able to let my body do its thing without fearing the pain.

Chase rubbed my feet, rubbed my back, propped my pillow, and watched a movie with me on his tablet. He's also given me more forehead kisses in the last few hours than I've ever had in my life. He called his family and our friends to update them, kept track of the overnight bag I packed, and didn't say a word about the amniotic fluid that leaked out of my pad and onto his car seat on the ride here. He even brushed my teeth for me this morning.

"Dad, do you want to put your hand on your son's head when he comes out?" Dr. Dewson asks.

"That's an option?" Chase asks, his eyes wild with fear and his voice husky.

I shrug as well as I can in my situation as I feel another overwhelming urge to push. "Up to you."

Chase finally glances down at where our child's head is crowning. His eyes widen like he's a character in a horror movie. The skin around his lips turns green, and I wonder if he'll pass out.

The big, strong police officer that does undercover drug bu sts....my ass.

He swallows and inhales through his nose before letting the doctor guide his hand to our child's crowning head. Chase blinks twice, looks up at me, nods like he's resigned to watching the miracle of birth, and looks down again.

Another urge to push moves through my body. I never understood what people in movies meant when they said that, but I get it now. Every muscle in my body screams for me to do something, anything, and pressure fills my entire stomach area. My toes curl into Chase's chest. My legs tremble, and my neck veins tighten as I push as hard as I can, blowing out a long grunt because even my lungs want to push something out.

Chase's eyes widen again, and his mouth opens in a large O. His eyes water, and I don't know if he's feeling empathetic over what's happening to my body or if he's seeing something cool.

Maybe a little of both, but I'm now regretting that I didn't take the nurse up on the offer of the mirror positioned so I could see my child born.

Chase is watching it, though, and that feels like it's enough somehow.

Something flops like a fish against my inner thighs and then a very messy human being is unceremoniously plopped onto my chest before I can blink or realize what's happening. Chase's hand is still on him. Maybe he isn't sure I'll react fast enough to grab hold of our child.

The red, squalling human with a clear resemblance to Chase around the brow line screams in terror, probably demanding to be put back where it's warm and not so bright. His eyes are open, blue, and search around the room in panic.

I should say something. He's my son.

"It's OK. Mommy's here."

It's the best I can manage. I didn't prepare a speech. I'm like an Oscar nominee who's shocked she won. I never thought I'd need to dazzle someone.

It's better than Chase's first words to our child, though. "Is his head going to fix itself, or is there something wrong with him?" Chase asks the nurse. I close my eyes for a moment and shake my head as the nurse assures Chase his child will not have a traffic-cone-shaped head for the rest of his life.

The baby looks at me, focusing for a brief millisecond when he hears my voice. He must recognize it since he's been inside of me for months. I can practically see the thought bubble above his head thinking, "Oh, there you are. You can't sing for shit, lady."

Chase cuts the cord, and the nurse dedicated to our son takes him from me to be weighed and measured. Chase stands nearby, obviously not sure what to do as his eyes bounce between me and our son. "Go with him," I urge.

Silently, Chase follows the nurse and watches from her side as drops are put into our son's eyes, he's cleaned, and a hat is placed on his little cone head.

"Now I know why babies always have hats on," Chase says. "It's because they have ugly heads."

I close my eyes and shake my head again.

The nurse gives him pretty much the same look. "Actually, sir, your baby is quite lovely. We put the hats on them because they can't regulate their body temperature like adults."

Soon enough, my son is back in my arms with a hat on. The nurse tending to him pulls down my hospital gown until the top of my chest is showing, and she places my son on me, then places a blanket on top of him. "Skin to skin is best to keep him warm. It'll also be good for him to smell you. If you're breastfeeding, you can try to start now. We'll give you a few minutes and then help you to the bathroom."

I nod as the entire medical team whisks out of the room, leaving me alone with Chase and a child I don't know but am now in charge of. Everything happens so fast when a child is born. The nurses certainly don't stand around impressed for very long. I guess when you see it every day several times a day, it's not so exciting.

Chase clears his throat and puts his hand on top of our son's head, stroking our unnamed child like he's glass. "That was scary, huh?" he asks. I'm not sure if he's asking me or our child.

"You're telling me. I'm still scared."

"Because we have to parent now?" he asks.

"I'm more scared because of what I've heard about peeing after giving birth."

"After what I just saw your body do, that's a legit fear, and I'm scared for you."

"Why are *you* scared?" I ask.

Chase kisses me on the forehead. "Because he's here now, and I'm nervous I'm not going to be a good dad. It felt real before, but now it's go time."

"What if we both suck?" I ask.

Chase looks at our child and a tear trickles down his face before he quickly wipes it away and smiles. "Then we'll suck together, I guess. We're in this as a family now no matter what."

"Funny that a meeting in a bar and a subsequent shag on the kitchen counter resulted in this," I say.

I pull my gown down to see if I can do the breastfeeding thing, and Chase even helps me as best as he can with our collective shit knowledge about breastfeeding. Eventually, our son finds my nipple and seems to be happy with it. I'll have the lactation consultant help me later. For now, our son isn't crying or fussing and seems content where he is, even if I'm not sure I'm giving him any food.

"Thanks for sticking by me," I whisper. "And you're already a good dad. I don't feel like a good mom, though. I don't feel like anyone's mom yet. Is that normal?"

"Yes. I read up on that a lot. Go at your own pace and do what feels right."

I smile at him, and he wipes a strand of hair back from my face. He did my hair twice tonight, pulling it into a ponytail for me when my arms were too hooked up to do it and then again when it came loose.

"You're not just a good dad, you're a good partner. I couldn't get through this without you."

He pushes his forehead to mine and closes his eyes. "You haven't left my mind since we met. You won't leave my mind until my brain shuts down with my dying breath. I love you, Kailee Lipshitz. I always will." He kisses my cheek and smiles against my jaw. "Maybe, when you're ready, we should also have a conversation about that last name of yours. That is, if you're tired of being called Shits."

THE END

***

Thanks for reading *Baked and Burned* and coming back to the *Contact High* world with me. Please leave a star rating or review on your retailer of choice. It helps me find other readers. If you'd like to follow me on social media for updates about new releases or sales, I'm at @authortoriross on Facebook and Instagram.

Also by Tori Ross

Romantic Comedy:

Contact High

Baked and Burned

The Cuffing Season Contract

The Panty Plot

All I Wank for Christmas

Winning the Witch

***

The Traveling Calvert Sisters Travel Novellas:

Head Over Heels in Hawaii

Loved in Las Vegas

Christmas on the Cruise Ship

Out of Luck in the Outback

Turkey in Tennessee
Lost in London

***

Why Choose:
Disco Bar
Techno Bar (coming soon)

***

Steamy Contemporary Romance:
Rocks

***

Superhero Romance
Arson
Thirst
Darkness
Amp

***

Erotica:

The Caretaker

The Substitute

The Progressive Dinner

Acknowledgements

This again. Look, I think I've thanked everyone I can thank in one of my previous books. I can only thank people so many times so I'll keep this brief.

Thank you to Deb for the proofreading. Thank you to Lee at Coffin Print Designs for this cover and the *Contact High* cover. Thanks for being so easy to work with.

Thank you to my author tribe: E.L. Koslo, Kelly Kay, Adonia Kane, Christian Pan, Samantha Baca, Indie Sparks, Evie Alexander, and Selena Moore. Thanks to Megan Kelly for always asking me how my day was when she sees me.

Thank you to my real life tribe for the support: Lisa, Nico, Jess, Jaime, Chrissy, and Paige. You all either buy my books or at least ask me how it's going. Thanks for the support and the venting sessions. Thank you to Kristie for the dick sweater.

Thank you to my readers of *Contact High* that looked forward to this book. I hope I didn't let you down, but damn, that was a lot of pressure.

Lastly, thank you to my husband and daughters for your endless patience with me.

About the author

Tori Ross is an Amazon bestselling and award-winning author of steamy contemporary romance and romantic comedy. Her book, *The Cuffing Season Contract*, won the National Indie Excellence Award for romantic comedy, and she's written several shorts, novellas, full-length books, and serials. She lives in Missouri with her family and two rescue dogs.